THE GREAT
KIDSBORO TAKEOVER

THE GREAT
KIDSBORO TAKEOVER

Marshal Younger

REVIEW AND HERALD® PUBLISHING ASSOCIATION
HAGERSTOWN, MD 21740

The author assumes full responsibility for the accuracy of all facts and
quotations as cited in this book.

This book was
Edited by Jeannette R. Johnson
Designed by Willie S. Duke
Cover art by Laura Stutzman
Typeset: 13/16 Bembo

PRINTED IN U.S.A.

04 03 02 01 00   5 4 3 2 1

R&H Cataloging Service
Younger, Marshal Scott, 1968–
    The great kidsboro takeover

        I. Title
            813.54

ISBN 0-8280-1427-2

*To Stephanie, who worked so
hard to keep a roof over our heads
while I sat at a computer and wrote
a bunch of stuff that will never sell
(and a couple of things that did).*

Rules, Rules, Rules!

No playing until your room is clean!
No dessert unless you finish the rest of your supper!
No jumping on the bed!

Does your family have some of these rules? Have you ever wondered why? A lot of the time we think that our parents make up rules just to take away our fun. But can you imagine a world without rules? What kind of people would we become if our parents let us steal, lie, and eat nothing but desserts? We would be dishonest, cheating, unhealthy people! Living by the rules when we are children helps us become responsible adults.

Ryan Cummings, mayor of the town of Kidsboro, also knows the importance of laws. At the beginning of this book, he tells us that he "runs a pretty tight ship," meaning that he doesn't let people get away with breaking the city's laws. There are a few people, like Valerie, who don't like all the rules in the city. As part of her run for mayor, she calls for fewer rules, and almost everyone in town jumps on the bandwagon. But as it turns out, Ryan is right about the town needing these rules.

Here are some questions to think about as you read this story:

What are some of the laws of Kidsboro and why are they needed? Why is it difficult to become a citizen of Kidsboro? Why does Ryan want it to be difficult? What happens when the rules of the town are ignored?

In the book of Exodus, you can read the story of how God led the Hebrew people out of the slavery of Egypt and set them on a journey to a new land of freedom—the Promised Land. This was a long, hard expedition with a crowd of hundreds of thousands of people. You can imagine how difficult it must have been to keep all of these people in order. God saw this, and so He gave His servant Moses a set of rules to give to the people. They were called the Ten Commandments. With these ten rules, God would teach His people how to live good lives.

When Jesus was on earth, He summed up all of these commandments in two sentences. You can read them for yourself in Matthew 22:37-38 (NIV):

"Love the Lord your God with all your heart and with all your soul and with all your mind. This is the first and greatest commandment." (Do this, and the first four commandments will fall into place.) "And the second is like it: Love your neighbor as yourself." (Do this, and the last six commandments will fall into place.)

Jesus believed in these rules, not because they were ways to keep us from doing what we want to do, but because they help us live our lives.

In Deuteronomy 6:2, 3 (ICB), Moses spoke for God, reassuring the Hebrews as they crossed over into the Promised Land: "Obey all his rules and commands I give you. Then you will live a long time. Listen, Israel, and carefully obey these laws. Then all will go well for you. You will become a great nation in a land where much food grows. The Lord, the God of your ancestors, has promised it to you."

That's some promise! And it's not one that God made just to the Israelites. He makes it to us too. If we read His Bible and obey His commands, we will be rewarded with a prosperous life.

Rules, rules, rules! Who needs 'em? *We all do!*

If I don't get what I want, I'm gonna take over this town and run you out," she said, smiling. The fact that she smiled was much worse than if she had frowned, or gritted her teeth. A frown would've meant she was serious about crushing me into tiny little bits. A smile meant she would also enjoy it.

My foot tapped nervously on the floor, but she couldn't see it because of the desk. I looked back at her, stone-faced. I hear that when faced with a vicious animal, you should never show fear. She would not see me flinch.

I'm the mayor and founder of Kidsboro, population 29. We're in Lake County, northeastern Ohio—a suburb of Cleveland. It's a nice little town—great place to raise kids. We have a church, a police station, a store, a bakery, a weekly newspaper, and big open spaces to play. Play is a key thing when 100 percent of the population is in the 7- to 14-year-old range.

My name is Ryan Cummings and I'm 12 years old. This probably raises the question, "How did a 12-year-old become the mayor of a town?" Well, it's not actually a town in the sense that you would find us on a map. It's a little place in the woods behind my house that my friends and I sort of took over. The "town" idea started as a school project two years ago and ended up as something we decided to do on our own. We all spend a lot of time there during the summer and after school during the rest of the year.

Everyone in our town has their own clubhouse. It isn't anything great. A box made of scrap wood that is just big enough for you to stand up in. In most of the clubhouses, you can touch opposite walls with both hands if you stretch out. Most people would call this small. I call it cozy.

Every citizen is also required to take their own place in society. I'm the mayor, but we also have a chief of police, three lawyers, a newspaper reporter, a number of small business owners, and others. It seems to work out pretty well. We started out as five people, and we've grown to 29. That's an average population growth of 290 percent per year, better than any major U.S. city. I think this is a good sign that we're doing something right.

As mayor, I run a pretty tight ship. We have a strict set of rules, and if anyone breaks them they can receive a fine, jail time (two hours is the maximum sentence), and, though it has never happened to this point, they can even be banished from the city. It is also quite difficult to become a citizen of the town. A person has to meet several standards before he or she will even be considered, and then it is still up to the city council to approve them.

Which was the reason why Valerie was glaring down at me with daggers for eyes. My authority as mayor was being challenged.

She stood up without taking her eyes off me. She leaned over my desk until her long brown hair was almost swinging in my face. "Ashley gets in," she said. She turned around and left, her work here done.

Whew! I could finally exhale. I wiped the sweat off my forehead with my sleeve and paced around the office, trying to work off some nervous energy. Most of the guys in our school, including me, actually admit to being afraid of Valerie. The guys who don't admit it are lying. Rumor has it that she actually made the football team's 240-pound starting left tackle wet his pants. I believed the rumor, and it's for one reason— she always gets what she wants. And why not? She's popular, pretty, and incredibly smart. She's been vale- dictorian of my school every year since the first grade. And crushing me under her cruel thumb would be as easy for her as crushing an ant with her foot.

This is why I was nervous. Valerie is a member of our town, and she wanted her best friend, Ashley, to get in as well. That afternoon Ashley's name would be reviewed by the city council for possible citizenship in our town. Valerie knew that the five council members had to vote on her. If Ashley didn't get an 80 percent majority vote (meaning four out of five people had to say "yes"), she didn't get in at all. Valerie knew she had three votes already. But mine was the deciding vote. If I voted yes to Ashley, she got in. If I voted no, she didn't.

The problem was, I didn't like Ashley. She's always been kind of mean to me, plus she gets into trouble a lot at school. I'd seen her cheat on tests and copy other people's homework assignments. This is not the type of person I want in my town. This is a community filled with good citizens who follow rules. And for the town to work, the rules have to be followed. After all, this is not a real city—we can't actually force anyone to pay a fine or stay in jail, so everyone has to follow the rules on their own. A person like Ashley wouldn't take the laws seriously. I knew that.

So here was my choice. I could put the town in danger by allowing a person in who would ruin it. Or I could put *myself* in danger by tugging on the chain of a fierce pit bull named Valerie.

Politics.

* * *

I went to the meeting hall, the largest building in Kidsboro. It was about three times the size of any of the clubhouses. If you squeezed in, all 29 citizens of Kidsboro could fit in, though only a few of them would get to sit. This is the place the city council meets to discuss things. It's also an entertainment center. We had a talent show here a few weeks ago. Marcy Watson won it by playing this song that she said was Mozart (though no one could really confirm this) on her baby brother's Donald Duck xylophone. It was unbelievable. She won a gift certificate from Sid's Bakery.

All five members of the council were gathered around a table. Two years ago this group came up with the idea of Kidsboro and made it into the town it is.

There was Scott Sanchez, my best friend. He's Spanish, though nothing about him is very Spanish except for his dark hair and dark skin. His father was born in Mexico, I think, but I guess that sort of thing must skip a generation. When I first met him and learned his last name, I tried to welcome him with a warm "Como estas?" He replied, "Huh?" Scott runs a detective agency here in town, though he's never gotten any cases in the two years he's been here. If he ever did get a case, I don't think he would have a clue how to go about solving it.

To Scott's left, Jill Segler was brushing her jet-black hair from her eyes. She's always doing that. She's the editor and only employee of the *Kidsboro Chronicle*, the town newspaper. It's a weekly that she prints on her Dad's computer. Unfortunately, there's not a lot of news to report in a town of 29—especially when the crime rate is basically zero. A donut was stolen from Sid's Bakery a few months ago, and Jill had a field day with that news. It was front page news for three issues. She did extensive interviews, photographs of the crime scene, feature stories on the history of the bakery, and the history of donuts and the history of stolen donuts . . . and then Sid remembered that he ate the donut. Jill got a lot of ribbing for that.

Next to her, Alice Funderburk is jerking her head back and forth to crack the bones in her thick neck. She's the chief of police. No one was ever brave enough to ask her how she could be the chief when there were no officers for her to be chief *of*. To question her on this would be unwise. She's a five-foot-eleven-inch seventh grader who outweighs the rest of the city council put together—and most of that is muscle.

Finally, Nelson Swanson spits on his glasses and wipes them with the corner of his shirt. He's Valerie's brother and her intellectual equal. But unlike her, he uses his intelligence for good instead of evil. He is actually an inventor of sorts. He has homemade, solar-powered air conditioning in his clubhouse.

They sit there, staring at me, knowing exactly what's going through my head. Ashley's future in Kidsboro, and possibly *my* future as a living, walking human being depends on my vote. Jill and Alice would vote for her, because Ashley always invites them to her birthday parties. Ashley lives on Lake Erie, and everyone can go boating, swimming, and water skiing. It's always the best party of the year. Jill and Alice would vote for her simply because they needed that invitation in their mailbox. Nelson would vote for Ashley simply in fear of his sister. Getting Valerie mad at *me* was one thing. But for Nelson to actually live with his sister every day in adjoining rooms where she has easy 24-hour access to his neck, would be a nightmare.

Scott would vote against Ashley. Ashley and Scott hate each other, and he would do anything to keep her out.

So the vote would be 3 to 1. If I vote yes, the vote will be 4 to 1, and Ashley will have the required 80 percent.

We went around the room.

"Yes," Alice said.

"Yes," Jill said.

"No," Scott said.

"Yes," Nelson said.

No surprises. They all looked at me. I could almost feel Valerie's hands around my neck, ready to squeeze. I took a long breath, still not quite sure what I was going to say. I closed my eyes tightly. Sweat began to trickle slowly down my face. Not a sound came from the other four members of the council as I open my eyes and let the word slide off my tongue.

"No."

CHAPTER 2

I remained seated as everyone filed out of the meeting hall past me. Nelson looked at me like a priest would look at a man who was about to be executed. He adjusted his glasses and put his hand on my shoulder as if to say "Bless you my son" and that he'd pray for my soul. Scott, being my best friend, probably thought he should be supportive, and so he said, "The town thanks you." But I think I heard him laughing as soon as he got outside. Jill smiled as if she might just have a homicide to report in the next edition of the newspaper. Alice offered her protection. I think she was joking, but I'm not sure.

I started out of the meeting hall myself. I expected Valerie to jump around the corner immediately, but she didn't. This frightened me. I figured I would be OK as long as I could look her in the eye. But if she lurked in the shadows, I'd probably go nuts. Maybe she knew this. Maybe her plan was to drive me crazy by *not* acting. It would certainly cause everyone in town to wonder whether or not they should have a mayor who was insane. Then, when she had everyone thinking I should be locked up, she would take over. That was her plan—and it was working rather well so far.

* * *

Scott and I walked back to the office. On the way we passed by Sid's Bakery, a little place in the middle of town where Sid brought in donuts, muffins, cookies, and sometimes cakes from home. He made them all himself, and almost always sold everything. He had one advantage in that kids are never too picky about freshness, so he could always sell a three-day-old donut. The bakery was not much bigger than a regular clubhouse, but he always had a table full of pastries inside. I hadn't been there in a while, and I thought a cinnamon raisin donut might be nice. But when we got there, Sid was leaving.

"Where are you going?"

"You're too late. I just threw away my last donut."

"You're closing already?"

"Yep. Forever."

Sure enough, there on the outside of the door was a sign he had posted that read: "Going Out of Business Sale. We had muffins, 2 for a charm. You should've been here."

We had our own currency in Kidsboro. A charm was like a penny. The charms were made out of cardboard circles and had a special ink imprint on them that only Jill had access to. She was in charge of printing all the money.

Sid's muffins were usually five charms each—and everyone in Kidsboro would agree that they were worth it. Most people in town had some vague idea about what they wanted to be when they grew up. But Sid didn't have just an idea, he had a destiny. At 13 he was a fine chef in the making. He was already better than my mom—not that my mom was a bad cook. He was just a master. A pastry artist. Closing his bakery was like Michelangelo deciding to go into real estate.

"Why are you shutting down?" I asked.

"It's not worth it. Nobody buys anything anymore."

"*I* was just coming to buy something."

"Great. But where have you been? You know how much stuff I sold last week? Two donuts, three cookies, and a bear claw. I can't survive on that."

"So what are you gonna do?"

"I don't know."

"You can't leave!" I shouted, sounding more desperate than I meant to. "Maybe it was just a slow week. People'll be back."

"I can't wait for that. I'm wasting too much good food."

"OK, OK. You can go for a while. Then everybody will miss you, and—you can come back."

"Maybe." And with a look that made me think that "maybe" meant "I'm going to France to find people who appreciate my talents," he left.

I looked at Scott. "I can't believe that. He had a great business. Did you ever try those bear claws? They're incredible."

"Nope. Never tried one. I never bought *anything* from the bakery."

"Why not?"

"I don't have any money."

This was true. Scott had never earned a dime with his detective agency. I immediately wondered if this was true of more people in Kidsboro. Everyone was responsible for making their own living, in whatever way they wanted. As mayor, I was paid by the city. This meant that every three months all the residents paid 10 percent of their income in taxes. This money went to pay me, Alice, and Corey, the garbage collector. All of us were "employed" by the city. Tax money also went to buy special buildings, like the meeting hall. So I never had to worry about making a living. Alice, in addition to being the police chief, was also in charge of collecting taxes. She was an obvious choice, because no one would dare try to cheat her, for fear of their very lives. Alice took care of all this herself, so I didn't know how much anyone made at all.

Were there a lot of people out there not making anything? Was that the reason Sid went out of business?

* * *

There were other matters at hand, though. City council needed another candidate to fill Ashley's spot. We had agreed a week before to increase the city's population by one. I was in charge of finding someone. I had been scouting out a boy named David for a few days and was ready to report my choice to Scott.

"There he is," I said to Scott as we ate lunch in the school cafeteria. I pointed to a boy sitting alone at the very last table. David always sat alone—I liked that about him, to be honest. I like unpopular people. People who were welcome members of our town were often people who were members of nothing else. David had no reason to be popular. He was plain looking, pretty boring in personality, and never got into trouble for anything.

"David Smith?" Scott asked. "Are you sure?"

"He's perfect," I said.

Scott dipped a French fry in his ketchup. "Pardon me for asking, but you *do* know the rumor about his dad, don't you?"

"Yeah, but even if it were true, which I doubt, what does that have to do with him?"

It was a popular rumor around school that David's dad was in jail. No one knew exactly why, but everyone had a guess. David denied all of it. I believed him, though I had no evidence on my side.

"So maybe we should ask him," Scott said, his

ketchup-laden French fry dangling limply from his hand.

"Ask him if his father's in jail?"

"Yeah. The city council's gonna want to know."

"Why should it matter?" I asked.

"I don't know. You don't think it matters?"

"No."

Family matters were private. I knew this, especially because I wanted my own family matters to be private. My mother was divorced right before we moved from California to Ohio. I was 8 then. No one knew anything about my life before I turned 8, and I was determined to keep it that way. It was something I never talked about, even with Scott. David had a right to keep his mouth shut too.

"Pardon me for breathing," Scott said, "but does he even wanna be in Kidsboro?"

"I told him about it," I said, "and he seemed to think it was a cool idea."

The next day I presented David to the city council and gave some arguments why I thought he should be a citizen of our town. He was a unanimous selection, even though no one really knew him. They all trusted my judgment.

I gave David the news, and he seemed happy about it. He knew nothing about the town, but was thrilled at simply being a part of something. We all knew the feeling.

I introduced him to the rest of the city council and a few others. I showed him his new house, gave him a copy of the city charter, and left him to decide what his place would be in Kidsboro.

* * *

On Thursday night there was a buzz in the air about some kind of meeting or rally or something that was taking place at the meeting hall. I figured I should check it out. When I got there, the place was packed. Almost everybody in town was crammed into the room.

Valerie stepped to the front and stood behind a music stand. Oh, no. It was Valerie's rally. I bit my lip to keep it from quivering as she began to speak.

"Here, I have the city charter," she said, holding up a 10-page booklet. "Let me read some of the rules we have in this town: 'No one is allowed to be in the city after 11:00 p.m. unless an overnight event is planned and approved by the city council.'" She flipped a page. "Here's another: 'There will be no fires or fireworks inside the city limits.'" She flipped through some more. Her eyes widened as though she saw a really offensive one. "And it goes on like this for 10 pages." She paused for dramatic effect. "Is it my imagination, or has our city council suddenly become our parents?"

Heads began nodding in approval. She continued. "These people think they can tell us how to live our lives. They don't think we have enough rules. But don't we? I mean, we have rules in school, we have rules at home, we have rules at church, on the street, and in the grocery store. We're kids! Shouldn't there be a place we can go where we are free to do what we want to do?"

More and more heads were nodding. She sensed that she had the crowd in the palm of her hand, so she raised her voice. "We don't need the city council and the mayor to be our baby-sitters!"

An unidentified voice shouted, "Yeah!" Most of the crowd was sitting high up in their seats, ready for a revolt. Four people were notably *not* sitting up in their seats. Me, of course, and three other members of the city council. Alice was the only member of the council who wasn't sinking down in her seat. She was standing in the front corner of the room with her hand on her hip (where a real police officer would have a gun), poised to extinguish a riot if she needed to.

Valerie was about to continue when someone burst in. "Hey, come on! There's been a break-in at Marcy's house! The new kid did it!"

Everyone rushed past me to see what all the excitement was about. I was the last one out of the hall.

* * *

When I arrived at Marcy's, the scene was clear. She was standing in the middle of her house, looking at all of her stuff. It looked as though it had been damaged by someone swinging a baseball bat. No one kept anything expensive in their house, but she had a chair, some pictures, a lamp, a few books, and a clock that were destroyed. Her wooden walls were cracked in several places as well. David was there too. Alice was searching him (just in case he was actually carrying a weapon). She had him standing straight up against the outside wall of the clubhouse, bending his arm across his lower back. She was reading him his rights (which she had memorized for just an occasion as this).

I went up to her. "What happened?"

"Marcy came home, and the door was wide open. The whole stinking place was trashed. And this little punk was standing here like the cat who ate the canary," Alice said, bending his arm farther toward his head. He winced.

"You saw David trashing your place?" I asked Marcy.

"No. But he was here. Standing right outside the door."

"David, were you in Marcy's house?"

"Yes," he said. "But—I-I didn't do it."

The crowd, all ready to hang somebody after Valerie's speech, didn't believe him. Alice took David away and put him in our jail.

The city charter states that if anyone is arrested for something, they must go to jail until an investigation can be completed. This was the first time in Kidsboro history that we'd had to look at this page of the city charter.

Alice would do the investigation, David would be put on trial, and then if he was found guilty, the city council would have to decide what the punishment should be. If David was convicted, there would be no other choice for us but to kick him out of town. This was a serious crime.

Alice looked over the crime scene, took statements from Marcy and David, and checked around to see if there were any other witnesses. There weren't. Things didn't look too good for David.

In fact, I was beginning to think he might actually have done it. I wanted to believe him but, frankly, all the evidence pointed in his direction. I went to the jail to talk to him.

He was obediently sitting in the cell, which was barely larger than a closet. The bars were made out of thin tree branches, and anybody with the strength of a kitten could get out of there, but the understanding was that you didn't try. I guess all of our rules were pretty much this type of understanding.

David barely looked up when I walked in. He acted like a guy who'd just missed a million-dollar free throw. He was that close. Ever since he moved into this area, he had been hoping for a chance to fit in somewhere. This was his chance, and it looked like it was slipping away.

I sat at Alice's desk outside the cell and looked into his eyes. He stared back at me blankly. I decided to be up-front. "Did you do it?"

"No," he said sincerely. He explained with a slight New York accent, "I was in my house, ya know, puttin' pictures up on my walls. Then I heard somebody call me. So I went to see who it was, and I saw Marcy's door open. I thought maybe the voice came from inside, ya know? So I went in and saw the whole place trashed. Next thing I knew, Marcy was there lookin' at me. She yelled. I didn't know what to do. I just stood there, then that big police girl came around and threw me against the wall."

"You said you heard somebody call out your name. Was it a boy's voice or a girl's voice?"

"Boy."

"Did you recognize it?"

"No."

"Did you tell Alice all of this?"

"Yeah. I don't think she believed me, though." He looked me straight in the face with puppy dog eyes and asked, "Do *you* believe me?"

It suddenly occurred to me that my opinion might be important to him. Maybe I was the only person who had ever given him a chance. Now my answer to this question would do one of two things: show me to be a true friend, or lump me in with all of the other kids who hated him because of his father's reputation. The way I answered was more important to him than being a part of the city. "Yes, I believe you," I said, and I think I meant it, but to be honest, I wasn't sure.

* * *

I was on my way to help Alice with the investigation when I saw a crowd of people gathered around Jill. She was holding up a newspaper, and everyone around her was waving their money around to get one. "Special edition! Ten charms a copy! Read all about the Kidsboro Bandit!"

The normal price for an issue of the paper was five charms. This was the biggest story ever to hit Kidsboro, so 10 charms was probably a bargain.

I went up to Jill and took 10 charms out of my

pocket. "How did you do this so fast?"

"Old news is no news. And this is the biggest story in the history of Kidsboro."

"Yeah, but how did you get all the information already?"

"You wanna know what made the front page of my last issue? Alice's new police badge that she bought at a carnival," she said, rolling her eyes. "Let's just say I was inspired."

I smiled, and looked at the story. She had certainly made headway in the past two hours. She had summaries, interviews, pictures of the scene (apparently she went to a one-hour photo place), biographies of all the people involved—wait a minute!

My face turned hot as I flipped to page two of the story. Jill had made her way down the street and was giving change to someone. I stormed after to her.

"What is this?" I said angrily.

"What?" she asked innocently.

"You mentioned David's father?"

"Yeah. Did you know his father's in jail?"

"First of all, that's a rumor. Second, how dare you *print* it!"

"It's a fact related to the story."

"It has nothing to do with the story."

"Don't you think it's important?"

"No, I don't!" I shouted. "It has nothing to do with whether or not he broke into Marcy's house!"

"He did it, Ryan. Everybody knows it."

"*I* don't know it. In fact, I'm beginning to doubt that he had anything to do with it. The point is, he hasn't had a trial yet. He's innocent until proven guilty in court."

She breathed heavily a few times, then realized she had no comeback.

"Don't tell me how to do my job!" She huffed, and charged off.

* * *

The trial process was a little sketchy, but we had it in the city charter. We had three lawyers. One was Pete Marvison, who liked the idea of being a lawyer and watched a lot of lawyer television shows but had no earthly idea how to be a lawyer. Unfortunately, Pete was David's lawyer. Worse yet, the prosecuting lawyer was none other than Valerie Swanson. *Pete vs. Valerie.* The David vs. Goliath of brains. But in this case, instead of a slingshot, David had, like, a wet noodle.

I really knew Pete was in trouble when he shouted "Objection!" before the trial even started. Amy, the judge, said, "What are you objecting to?" and Pete slid back down in his chair and sheepishly said, "Never mind."

Valerie spoke well. She used big words and even concepts like "reasonable doubt." She even spoke in Latin at one point, and I could tell this made an impact on the jury. Her first witness was Officer Alice. Alice obviously thought David did it. Later on, Valerie had the gall to mention David's father. I glanced at Pete, hoping for an objection, but he was sitting in his chair, trying to get chocolate off his sleeve.

Pete asked Alice a few questions too, but they were completely beside the point. He asked her if she really thought girls could be police officers. Alice and, well, pretty much everyone in the room was offended by this question. Alice rolled up her sleeves like she was going to deck him, but before she could, Pete quickly said, "No further questions, your honor," and backed away.

The five-person jury went outside to discuss the case, but everyone knew the case was already decided. They returned in 30 seconds to declare David guilty.

The city council voted 4-0 to throw David out of town. The missing vote was mine.

David was back in jail, where he was supposed to stay until the city council made their decision. Alice was watching him like a hawk, and I asked her if I could be alone with David for a minute. She glared at me as if to warn me not to try anything foolish, like helping him escape. But I gestured with my hands, assuring her that the thought would never cross my mind.

"You don't gotta tell me," he said. "I know how the vote went."

"I'm sorry," was all I could say. "You can come

on out of there if you want."

He stood up, and I let him out. He wouldn't look me in the eye.

"Hey," I said, "we're still friends, OK?"

He thought for a second, chuckled, then said, "Yeah, like we were even friends to begin with."

"We will be now."

He didn't believe me, but managed a smile anyway. "Sure."

I think he assumed that I would never talk to him again.

* * *

I was hoping to look further into the burglary, but I felt as though I had to get on with some mayoral duties first. I had several appointments on this day with the ones in town who I thought might be in the same predicament Scott was in—they had no money, because they didn't make any. There were several people in town I suspected started out broke and were still that way.

The first appointment was with a boy named James— a puny little kid, who was probably the only person in town who would lose to Scott Sanchez in a fight. He didn't have to duck his head as he came through the door into my office. He looked like he was there to see the principal after stuffing another kid's head into a toilet.

"Hi, James," I said, trying to set him at ease.

"Hi."

"Sit down." He sat. "I'm having meetings with a bunch of people today, just to get some idea how everything is going. How you like living here, how you like your job, whatever. I'm always trying to get ideas about how to improve things."

He seemed to loosen up a bit and I went on. "So how *is* everything going?"

"Good."

"You like being a citizen here?"

"Sure."

"How's your job going?" He looked at me as if I had just asked him why he didn't hand in last night's homework.

"Fine."

"What is it you do again?"

"I'm a doctor." This was the scariest thing I think I ever heard.

"Really. And—have you—treated anyone?"

"No."

I breathed a subtle sigh of relief.

"You know, I only do first aid, anyway. No surgery or anything."

"Of course."

"I figured this was the woods; somebody might get hurt. So I got this medical kit at the store. It's got bandages, antiseptic, stuff like that. And I took a CPR course too. I have a card in my house; I'm a certified CPR-giver."

"Congratulations."

"But nobody trusts me. A few people have gotten hurt, but they won't let me put anything on it, not even a bandage. You remember when Max fell out of that tree and hurt his ankle?"

"Right."

"I went over and tried to help him, but he wouldn't let me. He called me a quack and limped home."

"So you've never actually used any of your medical skills?"

"Just on the dummies at school."

"Then you've never made any money at all since you've been here."

"No."

"No side jobs?"

"No."

"So you've never *bought* anything in town?"

"No."

"Hmm." I tapped my lips with my pencil. "OK, James, that's all I need. If you ever have any suggestions for making the town better, just let me know, OK?"

"Sure." He turned around and left.

I wanted to think that James was not the norm. James was, anyway, a pretty lazy person. This was doubtless the reason why he chose to be a doctor, a job in which he would have to work only if some minor injury occurred. Surely the others would be vital participants in the town's economy.

I was wrong. All the interviews were the same. I talked to 10 people, and none of them had made a dime all summer. Six of the 10 had never made any money at all. I had to do something about this.

* * *

I told the city council what was going on, and they agreed that we needed to make a law that made sure everyone had a legitimate job. I made a proposal that we establish a law stating that every person had to make at least 50 charms a week, and if they failed to do so three weeks in a row, then they would lose their house for the rest of the summer. I thought this was tough, but fair. Making 50 charms a week was a cakewalk.

After some tough discussion, the city council voted four to one that we enact this law for the good of the people, so that what happened to Sid wouldn't happen again. Scott voted against it, undoubtedly because this meant he had to find a way to make some money himself.

I left the meeting feeling that I had accomplished something. The "Everybody Works" program seemed like a good long-term idea, even if it didn't win me any popularity contest at first. I was working for the good of the city.

* * *

A couple of days later, as I walked to my club-house office, I noticed Valerie and a few others gathered out front. It looked like a press conference. Jill was there, writing down everything Valerie said. The others were listening intently.

"I don't know about anyone else," Valerie said, "but I'm embarrassed for our mayor. What is this 'Everybody Works' program? Now he's *forcing* us to work? Don't we work enough at school and at home without having to worry about the daily grind in Kidsboro? This man is in love with rules. And another thing: he selected this David to be a member of our community, and not two days after he was voted in, he commits the biggest crime ever committed in Kidsboro. I'm beginning to think the mayor doesn't really know what's best for the city anymore."

Valerie spotted me as I was walking up. She smiled that evil smile of hers. "Well, hello, Mr. Mayor." Jill stopped writing and looked up at me as well. She smiled her own version of an evil smile. She obviously planned on printing Valerie's every word in the next issue.

Valerie continued the press conference. "As I was saying, I'm beginning to lose my trust in a mayor who votes to have criminals put on our streets."

I turned away, realizing her vision to destroy me was only just beginning.

Suddenly it dawned on me. Of course! Valerie wanted to disgrace me in front of the whole town. What better way to do it than to disgrace one of the people I chose to join the town! Valerie had set David up! I ran toward my office. The investigation was now reopened!

The police had already declared that the investigation was over, so I couldn't ask them for help. I decided to go to the only other place in town—the Scott Sanchez Detective Agency. I realized he had never been hired before, but another set of eyes and brains wouldn't hurt, no matter how well-trained the eyes and brains were. Plus, I promised Scott after we enacted the new law that I would help him find work. Keeping my promises . . . What an elected official I am!

When I walked through his door, he was sitting in a lawn chair, reading a book. It never even occurred to him that I might be a customer. "Hey," he said. "What's up?"

"I'm here to hire you," I said.

"You what?"

"I want to hire you."

"Pardon me for being dense, but I don't follow."

"Aren't you a detective?" I asked.

"Sure."

"I need a detective."

He dropped the book as if his hands had suddenly gone numb. He had no idea what to do at this point. I could almost see his brain whirling. Should he ask a bunch of questions? Should he get his magnifying glass? Should he take my fingerprints?

"How much do you charge?" I asked as I pulled a few starbills out of my pocket (a starbill was equal to 100 charms).

Scott was clueless as to what he charged. "How much? Um—I don't know. I—I used to have this written down somewhere. Pardon me." He began to rummage through a shelf. It was filled with books, cereal box tops, and a paddleball game. You know—all that important detective equipment. He stopped looking and faced me again. "I'll tell you what. Since you're a friend, I'll forget the rates and give you a discount."

"Sounds fair," I said, knowing he was winging this.

"How about a starbill an hour?"

This rate was a little steep, but I thought I'd give him a break. "It's a deal."

"Great. OK." He nervously looked around, hoping by some miracle that there might be something lying around his office that would tell him where to start.

"Listen," I said as he continued to search. "I don't think David broke into Marcy's house. I think we should reopen the investigation."

"Here it is," he said triumphantly. He held up a plaid hat, like the one Sherlock Holmes wore. He returned to his shelf. I prayed silently that he wasn't searching for his pipe.

"Great. Did you hear me?"

"Yes. Marcy's house. Who do you think did it?"

"I have my suspicions, but I'd rather not say right now."

"OK," he said. I waited for him to suggest a course of action, but I was torn. I wanted to give him the chance to lead the investigation, but at the same time he was charging me a starbill an hour for this. I wanted to get started on it.

"Why don't we go to David's old house?" I said finally.

"Good idea." He started out the door.

"Um," I said, "are you going to wear that hat?"

He stopped and thought about it. "You don't like the hat?"

"It's just—a little—goofy."

He seemed offended, and for the first time showed me who was boss here. "I'm leading this investigation, thank you. Come on."

* * *

David's house had been left just as it was when the burglary took place. He hadn't come back for any of his stuff. He probably didn't want to risk running into anyone and having to explain himself. There were magazine pictures scattered all around.

"Wait a minute," I said. "He told me he was putting up pictures when he heard someone call his name."

"That looks possible," Scott said. "Some of these pictures are tacked up, some aren't." This was obvious to both of us, but since I was paying him, I guess he felt he ought to observe something.

We continued looking around, but we were interrupted by some breaking news. Alice ran up to us with a frown.

"There's been another break-in."

* * *

It was Nelson Swanson's house. The place was littered with blueprints, ideas, sketches, and a number of different gadgets that Nelson had invented. It looked like someone had trashed it just for the sake of trashing it. Alice pointed up. "Hole in the ceiling. Looks like that's the way the wormball got in."

"Did anybody see anything?" I asked Alice.

"No," Alice replied, having a little trouble concentrating on my question because she was distracted by Scott's hat. "Nelson says nothing was stolen."

"Now why would somebody go to all the trouble to break through the ceiling, trash the whole place, and not steal anything?"

"I don't know." She raised her eyebrows as if

she *did* know. "Revenge, maybe?"

"You think it was David?"

She lowered her voice. Scott, who was listening up to this point, backed away, because he sensed he wasn't invited to the conversation. "A professional did this. They knew what they were doing. And David's father being who he is—"

"I don't want to hear anymore!" I said angrily. She was jumping to a wild conclusion, and she knew it.

"Where's Nelson?" I asked.

She pointed outside. Nelson was sitting by a tree, looking troubled and holding a metal gadget. "You OK, Nelson?" I asked.

"Fine."

"What's that?"

"A broken automatic door opener. I was so close to perfecting it. All I had to do was adjust the sensitivity—"

"Nothing was taken, right?"

"No," he said. "Actually, though—" He stopped for a second and looked at Scott. "Why is he wearing that hat?" he asked, as if a person wearing this hat couldn't possibly be capable of answering for himself.

"I don't know," I said.

Nelson shook it off. "As I was saying, it's strange, because I invented a burglar alarm several months ago and the entire room was wired. I can't fathom why it didn't work."

A Southern voice came out of nowhere. "Kinda makes you wonder if *anybody's* safe, doesn't it?"

I looked up and saw Max Darby. Max was one of two African-Americans in Kidsboro. He had moved up from Georgia a few years ago and hadn't even begun to lose his accent. If anything, it seemed to have gotten thicker since he came to Ohio. Max was one of the first people accepted into town by the city council. He was chosen because his father owned a construction company, and his dad gave him unlimited amounts of scrap wood. So Max was the reason we all had houses.

Max always seemed to be up to something. He would like you to think he's your best friend, and everybody's best friend, but his real best friend was himself. Max was the richest person in town, because he had a product that everyone wanted—wood. He sold it for very high prices. I wouldn't want to guess how many starbills he had hidden away at home.

"You know what you need, little buddy?" Max said. "You need something that'll keep you high and dry when the rest of the world is floatin' down the river."

"What're you talking about?" Nelson asked.

I wished he hadn't.

"I'm talkin' peace of mind. Restful nights. I'm talkin' about preparin' for the future."

"OK, sure, but—what, *specifically,* are you talking about?"

"Insurance. The one thing that'll help you out if this ever happened again—"

"Max," I interrupted, "this isn't the time."

"Oh, I disagree. I think this is the perfect time."

Nelson said, "Go on."

Max knelt down next to Nelson and put his hand on his shoulder. He had him. "You'll never have to go through this again if you have Darby Insurance. Buy one of my policies at my limited time, special-price offer, and if tragedy ever strikes again, I'll pay you enough money to fix all the damages."

By the time Max was through with him, Nelson had bought a homeowner's policy. The way it worked was that Nelson paid Max a starbill every month, and if something ever happened to the house again, Max would pay to get everything replaced. Leave it to Max to make money from tragedy.

But to be honest, insurance wasn't such a bad idea for Kidsboro. In fact, Marcy, with her trashed house, probably wished she had insurance as well.

When a person was approved to become a citizen, they were given a certain amount of money with which to begin. Most people used this money to buy wood from Max and build their house. But there was nothing in the city charter that gave any money to people to help repair damage done to houses. So if something happened to your stuff, basically, you were stuck. You had to come up with your own money somehow. Now, if you bought Max's insurance, Max would take care of all of it. Apparently, a lot of people saw the benefits of it. Max sold five policies right there at the scene of the crime. He sold one to Scott, and told him his hat would be insured as well. I didn't buy one, simply on principle. I wasn't about to give my money to Max.

While Max introduced Scott to the details in his new policy, I sat under a tree and thought about the situation. The break-in just didn't make sense. If Valerie were responsible for the first break-in, why would she do this one as well? She would risk getting caught, and she had already made her point. Everyone in town thought David was a crook and that I was wrong for selecting him. She got me. So why would she do it again?

After the crowd had thinned out around Nelson's house, Scott and I quietly went back in to look around. Alice had gone somewhere, and I thought it would be the perfect opportunity to do some investigating myself.

The place was trashed in an unusual way, but it was hard to put my finger on what was so strange about it. I asked Scott what he thought, and of course he detected nothing.

"So they broke in," Scott began, knowing that detectives on TV always try to sum up the case every now and then. "Through the roof. Knocked over the chair, broke a few gadgets, laid these books down on the table, threw a couple pieces of paper around—"

"Wait a minute!" I shouted. "That's it!"

Scott was pleased that his summary seemed to have helped jar something in my brain. "What?"

"These books—look at 'em! They're laid down

on the table like somebody was getting ready to study. If someone were coming in just to make a mess, wouldn't they be thrown everywhere—on the floor, lying open? And look at this chair! It looks like it was carefully laid down on the dirt." I was on to something. "Get Nelson!"

Scott left to earn some of his money and came back with Nelson.

"Nelson, were these books already laying on the desk like this?" I asked.

"No, I always put them up on this shelf. I assume the burglar did that."

"Tell me about your alarm system," I said, playing a hunch.

"Well . . . I set up wires around the room, on the walls, around the circumference of the window there. And if someone bumps it, it releases a high-pitched noise. Pretty much everybody in town would be able to hear it."

"Is there any way somebody could've gotten in here and not tripped the alarm?"

"No. The alarm must have malfunctioned—or maybe I forgot to turn it on; I don't know."

"What if they came through the roof?"

"Well, sure, I didn't have any wires on the ceiling. But if somebody came in here and was throwing books and stuff around, there's no way they wouldn't hit an alarm somewhere."

"But that's just it," I said. "These books are *not*

thrown around. Look at this chair: it's laid down so nicely, not touching any walls, not tripping any alarms."

Nelson was beginning to see where I was going with this. Scott still didn't have a clue. "You're right," Nelson said. "So whoever broke in must've known where the alarms were set."

"Exactly," I said. "Did anyone besides you know where you put the alarms?"

"Well . . ." Nelson began thinking. "I've had people in my house before. I suppose someone could've noticed where the wires were."

"Who?"

"Well . . . You."

Scott suddenly woke up. "You're accusing Ryan?"

"No. I'm just trying to think who's been in here. My sister . . ."

This one caused my eyebrow to raise a little.

"Oh, Nick was in here once."

This was odd. Nick and Nelson were far from being friends. Nick was the handyman of the town. His father worked in a tool shop, and he knew how to build clubhouses and just about anything else.

"Nick?" I asked.

"Yeah, he—" Nelson looked at us like the mystery was suddenly solved. "He helped me put in the alarm system."

"How?"

"He stapled the wiring to the walls. He knows the whole system—where all the wires are placed and how much pressure is needed to set them off. He knows everything!"

I looked at Scott. He said, in perfect TV detective fashion, "I think we need to take a little trip to Nick's house."

There was a knock at the door. It was Alice.

"Nelson, I need to take an official statement—" She stopped suddenly when it dawned on her why Scott and I might be in the room. "What are you guys doing here?"

"We're just, um—" I began, not sure if I should tell her. "We're talking to Nelson."

"About what?"

"Nothing," Scott said quickly, telling Alice immediately that we were, indeed, talking about something. Scott's knees began shaking.

Alice looked at Scott. "Does that hat mean you're doing detective work?"

"Well, I—"

She looked at me. "This is *my* investigation, Mr. Mayor."

"Look, Alice . . . I just have this hunch—"

"And you think your hunch is better than mine?" Her neck muscles tightened in anger. Scott started to sway as if he was going to faint. "You think you can do this better than me?"

"I'm just—" I began. "No."

"Didn't think so. Now go do some mayor work."

Scott was out of the house in about three

milliseconds. I followed him.

* * *

On the way to Nick's house, Valerie stopped us. "Mr. Mayor, how lovely to see you," she said. Scott had taken enough ribbing about the hat and had taken it off by this point. "And you have your little elf with you too. How nice."

"We're kind of in a hurry, Valerie. Did you want something?"

"I just wanted to invite you to my press conference. I'm holding it in the meeting hall in about 10 minutes."

"You mean you have something *else* to say to the newspaper?"

"Oh, something very important," she said with that evil smile.

"What is it?"

"I'm running for mayor."

The city charter had nothing in it about how often elections were to be held. I had been the mayor since the beginning of the town, and nothing about the length of my term was ever made clear. So Valerie was completely right when she said she could run for mayor against me. This was as good a time as any for an election, I suppose—at least until we got something in the charter about it.

If the election were held that day, I figured I would beat her. Not to brag, but people in the town trusted me. Besides, I was the one who gave them their start. They were citizens of this town because of me. And with the exception of the serial burglar and Sid's Bakery closing, everything had run pretty smoothly from the beginning.

However, Valerie wasn't through campaigning, and something told me she was saving her best for last. She told me she was scheduling a debate. That would be a challenge for me. She had a way with words. I knew she could manipulate people, one-on-one, so I assumed she could do it with a crowd.

One thing that would really help me in the election would be to solve this burglary case and clear David's name. At least I wouldn't be accused of allowing criminals into town. It would be a bonus if I could link Valerie to the break-ins.

So I had a job to do. I needed to focus my attention on the one person who could get me out of this jam—Nick.

* * *

Nick was outside in his T-shirt and overalls, busily putting on an addition. Most people built small houses to begin with—about six feet wide by six feet long by six feet high—then, if they saved their money, they added on. They put on extra rooms, built extra tables, added shelves, and so on.

Max Darby, the guy with all the wood, had the biggest house in Kidsboro. He had four rooms, including a rec room that actually had a working air hockey table. Nelson helped him invent it. They poked holes in a sheet of heavily waxed wood and put a fan underneath it so the air would come out. It worked OK, but it took a while to get the bugs ironed out. One time the puck caught too much wind and flew off the table, smacking the town minister in the forehead. There was a circular mark on his forehead for about a week, and of course there were a lot of Anti-Christ jokes made.

Nick had knocked out part of a wall and was putting on a new room when we walked up.

"How's it going, Nick?" I asked.

"Pretty good."

"Looking great," I said. And it was. Nick was good at one, and only one, thing: building. He wasn't one of the smarter people in town. In fact, he was probably the only one in town who might actually lose a case to lawyer Pete. I thought I might be able to trip him up somewhere along the line.

I decided not to waste any time. "Did you hear there was another break-in?"

"Yeah, I heard something," he said.

"Nelson's house."

"That's too bad," he said, not looking up from a board he was hammering.

"Burglar got right past his alarm. Can you believe that?"

"Pretty wild."

"It almost seemed like the burglar knew exactly where the alarm was set."

"Really?" he said, making great efforts not to look at me.

"Nelson said that when he installed the alarm system you helped him with it."

He paused before he answered. "I don't know

what you're talking about."

Ah! He denied it. Now we were getting somewhere. "So you didn't help him with it?"

"No."

"Have you ever seen Nelson's system?"

"No."

"Have you ever been in Nelson's house?"

"No."

"Did you ever talk to Nelson at all about his alarm system?"

"No. Look, I don't care anything about Nelson. I've got nothing to do with any of this. I've been working on my house all day." Annoyed, he sent a nail all the way in with one hit of his hammer.

"But—"

"Just get outta here!" he interrupted. "I'm not answering any more questions."

I was satisfied with this meeting. I had obviously rattled him, and this made me pretty certain he was guilty. I was confident I could get proof somewhere along the line. I started to back away and leave.

"Pardon me for being born, Nick, but I don't believe you," Scott suddenly said.

I was shocked that Scott even spoke, much less say something aggressive. Scott continued, stammering nervously. "Nelson said that you—he said you helped him with his alarm. Then—then you're saying he's lying?"

"Yeah. He's lying."

"You didn't?

"What?"

"Help him?"

"No."

"Well, you see, I don't understand something. P-pardon me for intruding, but"—Scott walked over to a roll of electrical wiring that had been placed on a stump—"we found this same type of wire in his house."

"You can get that wire anywhere. He probably bought it in a store." This was a perfectly good answer, but it looked as if Nick was beginning to come unglued. For the first time, Nick was no longer paying attention to his hammering and was paying attention to Scott. Somehow, Scott sensed he was getting to him. A confidence came to his eyes.

"You know, you should've seen how well this alarm was placed in a hole in the wall. It was right there—it looked like a professional did it. With professional tools," Scott said, holding up a battery-operated power saw. "Kinda, well, kinda like this one."

I wanted to applaud.

Nick brushed a sweat drop from his forehead. "Lots of people have power tools."

"Wow! Look at this!" Scott said, holding up a screw. "We found these very same screws in Nelson's house."

"Ha! That's a lie!" Nick shouted. "His walls are too thick for that type of screw."

"But I thought you said you've never been in Nelson's house."

Bravo! Scott looked at Nick, who was breathing hard and thinking harder.

"Well, maybe I did go in there once. I don't remember."

"You're saying you remember what type of wood he has for his walls, but you don't remember if you actually stepped foot in his house."

"OK, I've been in his house a couple times. He's invited me in—"

"So you're friends?"

"Yeah, sure."

"But I thought you said a couple minutes ago that you didn't care anything about Nelson."

My chin had dropped to the ground about two minutes before, but now the rest of my body was about to join it. Scott was amazing. Perhaps endless hours of tough-guy detective shows had finally paid off for him.

Scott grilled him for a while longer until finally Nick got sick of getting caught in lies and confessed to breaking into Nelson's and Marcy's houses. He also confessed to setting up David. I told him that he would probably be kicked out of town for this. He acted like he didn't care.

Scott and I walked away. I was like a proud father. He seemed unaware that he had just done something incredible. He casually told me that he needed to go home for dinner. But as he walked away, I spotted him putting his hat back on and strutting like a victorious soldier.

* * *

Something still bothered me, though. I couldn't understand why Nick would do this. Scott tried to grill him on this too, but by that time Nick had had enough and wasn't about to answer any more questions. What possible reason would he have for breaking into two houses and not taking anything?

This, of course, led me back to Valerie. Did she hire him? I could understand the first house—she was trying to frame David to make me look bad. But the second house made absolutely no sense. But she *had* to have done it. Who else would have anything to gain by breaking into two houses?

Suddenly, like a message from above, I got my answer. As I was walking back to my office, I spotted Max Darby, a crowd of people around him, selling insurance. I was pretty sure this didn't happen in real life—an insurance salesman having to fight people off.

Of course! Max was getting rich because people were scared of being robbed! *Max* had something to gain! Max paid Nick to break into the houses! This would explain how Nick got the money and the wood to build a huge addition to his house. That's it! It's an insurance scam!

After the crowd around Max dwindled, I approached him. "Selling a lot of policies?"

"Fourteen, total," he said. "Seems to be the hot item. Wanna reconsider?"

"No, thanks. I'm sure glad someone is benefiting from this rash of crime."

"Oh, I'd never want to benefit from something like that."

"I'm sure you wouldn't," I said, knowing full well he would love to benefit from something like that. "I just found out who did it."

"Well, partner, I think you're a little late. Everybody else in town's known for days. It was that David kid you brought in."

"No, it wasn't." I paused for effect here. I wanted to be able to read guilt in his eyes, so I watched closely as I laid the bomb on him. "Nick did it."

He didn't flinch, blink, or blush. "Really? Never woulda suspected. Good guy, that Nick. Quiet, shy type. That's always a good type of person to sell insurance to."

I could suddenly picture Scott and his merciless grilling of Nick, and I decided to go in for the kill. "You paid him to do it."

Max smiled and chuckled a little, as if the thought never occurred to him. I expected him to deny it, but instead he offered a much more interesting idea. "Prove it," he said.

He had me there. I could accuse him all I wanted to, but unless Nick admitted it to me, point-blank in front of witnesses, I had no case.

Max took another unexpected turn. "Now, I know you didn't mean that. You're just fishin', I know. But let's pretend for a second that I *did* commit this tragic crime. What, exactly, can you do about it? Kick me out of town? I know how politics is, and banishing your most valuable citizen doesn't look too good, come election time."

"You think you're our most valuable citizen?"

"Where else you gonna get wood, buddy? You banish me, and I have every right to pull apart all these houses. This is *my* wood. And you know, it's real cute to see you acting like this is some kind of great democracy you're runnin' here. But when it all comes down to it, this town is just a bunch of clubhouses in the woods. You lose me, you got nothing." He smiled again and turned away. I watched him walk quickly and knock on a door. He had insurance to sell.

I went back by Nick's house. He was cleaning up his things, figuring that he was going to be kicked out of town. I talked to him for a while, but he would never admit to being hired by anyone. He had learned his lesson from the last time and wouldn't answer any of my questions with anything more than "No" or "Yes." I told him I would ask the council not to banish him if he would tell me who had hired him, but he wouldn't budge. He said he wasn't a rat. This was, of course, evidence that he had someone he could be ratting on.

But I still had no proof.

* * *

We held a city council meeting after school the next day. Jill, Nelson, Alice, and Scott filed in. Everyone knew why we were there: to discuss Nick's punishment. A trial wasn't necessary since he had confessed in front of two of us. After a short discussion we voted unanimously that Nick had to be dropped, and that David would be cleared of all charges. Alice felt quite embarrassed by the whole thing since this meant she had put an innocent man in jail. But she had no debate. She had made a mistake and was ready to move on. I think she was still mad at me.

Before everyone got to their feet, I stopped them, because I had something else to bring up. I wanted to vote on the punishment of Max Darby.

"What?" Jill asked, speaking for the whole crowd.

I cleared my throat to show them I was serious, then said, "I have reason to believe Max hired Nick to break into the houses so he could sell insurance policies."

They stared at me in disbelief. Finally, Jill was able to speak. "Do you have proof?"

"Well, no. But I'm pretty sure about it."

"Did he confess?"

"No."

"Well, we can't banish him just because you *think* he did it."

I was losing them. "I'm asking you to trust me."

Alice shook her head like I was crazy. "Sorry, Ryan. No can do. Not without a trial."

That's what I wanted them to say. "What if I get him to trial? Let me tell you why I think he's guilty. You tell me if you think he'll lose in court—"

"Wait a minute; wait a minute!" Jill interrupted. "I don't wanna hear this."

"Why not?"

"I don't want you bringing him to trial. What if he's found guilty?"

I was confused by the question. "Well, then justice would be served."

"Would we banish him?"

"Sure, I guess."

"Then where would we get our wood?" she asked, as if this was an obvious downfall.

Alice and Nelson nodded in agreement.

My heart sank. I never expected this from anyone in my city council—to place more value in wood than in justice.

I had a thousand responses, but could speak only one word. "Wood?" I asked weakly.

Jill continued. "I mean, I'm all for justice being served and all that, but if we banish Max, we're in deep trouble. We can't build anything. We can't add to the population. We have to think about the future of the town."

"The future of the town?" I asked in disbelief. "What kind of future are we going to have if people like Max know they can get away with stuff like this? What happened to our laws? Who cares about the quality of our houses? What about the quality of our people?" This was a great line, and if I hadn't been trying to make a point, I would've written it down and saved it for the debate.

Jill thought about it for a minute, but then shook her head. "Maybe we should let this one pass. Sorry, but like it or not, we *need* Max."

"She's right," Alice said. "I hate crime, but we gotta have wood."

Nelson nodded along with her, and Scott had been completely without commitment since the moment I started talking. My mouth hung open in disbelief. I had nothing else to say. I turned around and, with my head buried into my chest, left.

I talked to David the next day at school and told him he was welcome to come back into town. He was hesitant, saying that he didn't feel comfortable there right now. I could tell it hurt him that people jumped to the conclusion that he was a criminal. I understood, and said that I'd be back to ask him again soon.

The election was in a couple weeks, and I felt that the past week had been a definite victory for me. I was right about David. My approval rating was probably up, and Valerie had lost her whole he's-letting-criminals-into-town argument. So even though I was disappointed in my city council, I had something to keep my head up about.

I was headed over to Jill's office to see how she was planning to cover the Nick/David story in the newspaper, when I heard two angry voices coming from inside. I rushed to see what was going on. I opened the door to discover that it was just Jill and her friend Marcy. Marcy had one hand on her hip, and was using the other hand to shake a pencil in Jill's face.

"You just think you're Miss Journalism, don't you?" Marcy said, not seeing me yet.

"I'm not running your story. That doesn't mean I won't run other stories."

"It's a perfectly good story."

"There are finally some things going on in this town. We don't need fluff. Nobody cares about your canary." Jill glanced over to me. "Ryan, do you care about Marcy's canary?"

I'd seen Marcy's canary. It was cute. Would I throw myself in front of a bus for Marcy's canary? No. But do I *care* about it?

"Are you gonna answer the question, Ryan?"

"Oh. Uh, I don't know. Why?"

"Well, you see, Marcy's my new assistant. I'm paying her 50 charms a week so she can keep her house."

Hey! The "Everybody Works" program in motion!

"So I told her to write a story. Well, she came back with a story that I don't think works very well for our newspaper."

"But it's great! It could become a regular column— 'Citizens and Their Pets.' I think Nelson and Valerie have a Siamese cat."

"Great. We'll make it a double issue."

"This is not the New York *Times*. We're kids."

"It's lame, Marcy."

"It's not. And even if it was, so what? At least it fills up space."

"Let me explain something to you," Jill squared her shoulders as if she was about to teach her pupil something. "There are only two ways that this newspaper makes money—people who subscribe to it, and people who advertise in it. OK, right now I have eight subscribers and one advertiser—those scary insurance ads Max puts in. Now if any of those people decide that your canary story is too lame for them to keep spending money on this newspaper, I'm doomed. Do you understand?"

Marcy's shoulders fell. She wasn't mad, merely disappointed. "Fine. I'm leaving. Maybe somebody'll murder me on the way home, and you can have your great story." Marcy left.

Jill turned away from me and crumpled up the piece of paper in her hand. "Maybe we should rethink this 'Everybody Works' thing. I didn't know it would cause this."

"You don't think she'll work out eventually?" I said.

"She's a really good friend . . . but she doesn't have a clue about the newspaper business."

"Then why'd you hire her?"

"I had to. She was desperate. She didn't want to lose her house. So she came to me. I couldn't turn her down. She's my friend." She sighed, then an idea popped into her head. "I want to have another city council vote. On the 'Everybody Works' thing."

"We can't back out on it yet. Just give it a little time. It'll work." Little did I know that the problems between Marcy and Jill were only the tip of the iceberg.

* * *

"Everybody Works Doesn't Work," part two, occurred the next day when I ran into Pete the lawyer, and Nelson. Nelson was walking quickly, trying to get away from him, but Pete kept up the pace, throwing his face in front of Nelson to force him to make eye contact.

"But how do you *feel* about the break-in?" Pete asked

"I don't feel anything," Nelson said impatiently. "It just happened; they already caught the guy. It's over."

"But don't you feel emotional distress or anything?"

"No. Now go away."

I was terribly confused by this conversation.

"What about future stress? Do you think you'll have to go into therapy because you'll never feel safe in your own home again?"

"Listen, I'm working on a spanking machine, and I won't hesitate to make you my first guinea pig."

"What's going on?" I asked.

"He's trying to get me to sue somebody. But

there's *nobody to sue.*"

Pete was unmoved by my presence. "OK, let's forget the break-in. What about your life? Has there been anybody who discriminated against you recently? Maybe they defamed your character?"

"I'm in middle school. Everyone defames my character."

Pete's eyes lit up. "OK, OK! Now we're getting somewhere."

"Forget it, Pete."

I stepped in. "Look. There's no place for this. We can't have lawsuits against each other."

"Can I sue the government?"

"No."

"Well, what else am I supposed to do? I've never made any money by being a lawyer. Now because of this wonderful new law you've passed, I have to find a way to make some or I lose my house."

"There are better ways than this."

"I'm a lawyer, Ryan. I love the law." I could tell he got that line from a TV show, as well as the next one. "If I do anything else, it's like cheating on my girlfriend."

I rolled my eyes. Pete remained undaunted and looked at Nelson. "Now are you gonna listen to me or not?"

"No."

"You're missing out on almost certain riches, my man." Pete nodded his head sympathetically, then took off to chase after some more ambulances. I looked sheepishly at Nelson.

"I should've seen this coming," Nelson said. "And you know what? There are three lawyers in this town, two of whom have never made any money. Somebody's gonna end up suing. And if it works, it's gonna be a litigation free-for-all."

Something told me Nelson was right.

I sat in my office, banging a pencil against my card table desk. History is filled with leaders having to make tough decisions under pressure. I'm sure plenty of people asked George Washington, "Why are we crossing the Delaware? It's a dumb idea to cross the Delaware. Let's just go around the Delaware."

I picked up a pen and began to drum it against the desk as well. I knew that nobody would blame me if I decided to change my mind about the law. If I took the idea back to the city council, they'd choose to forget the "Everybody Works" program ever happened. The town wasn't too thrilled with it—I knew that. But I also believed it would work, over time. In three months, when the economy was back to normal, people would be telling me what a brilliant idea it was.

The thought passed through my brain that I could take back the new law, get reelected, then pass it again. But I knew that wouldn't be right. Maybe I could get reelected just on the basis of my integrity—the fact that I wouldn't take back the law, even if it meant losing the election. George Washington stuck to his guns. So could I. Maybe people would reelect me because of that.

Fat chance.

Jill burst in without knocking. I jumped a little when she slapped a piece of paper down on the desk in front of me.

"I'm being sued!"

"What?"

"Yesterday's issue had an interview with Corey Hawkins." Corey was the neighborhood garbage collector. "You know how Corey wants to start having recycling bins in town."

"Right."

"So I let Marcy do the interview. And she writes in the article that after he picks up our garbage, he uses some of it to decorate his room."

"What?"

"Exactly what I said. I asked her, 'Are you sure he told you that he decorates his room with garbage?' I asked her that three times. She swore up and down that that's what he said. So I do what you told me to do—I figured I would give her a shot. I ran with the story. Well, as it turns out, Corey doesn't decorate his room with garbage. He simply *knows* someone that decorates his room with things that other people would *consider* garbage."

"That's a pretty bad misquote."

"Apparently Corey's now the laughing stock of the town. He told me that one kid gave him a moldy donut and a nail and asked him if he wanted to hang it on his wall."

"So he's suing for libel."

"And he's got a case."

"For how much?

"Thirty starbills. I don't have it."

"I can't believe this."

"Do I have the authority to call a city council meeting?" she asked without hesitation. She had obviously already given this some thought.

"I'll talk to Corey. I'll ask him not to sue."

"That's not the point. This program isn't working. It's making people too desperate for money."

I breathed a long sigh and leaned back in my chair. She was making a good case. "I'll look into it." She gave me a long hard stare like she didn't believe me, nodded her head, and left without a word.

* * *

It was time for some more appointments. When in doubt, make an appointment. I needed to find out if this program was working at all. So I spoke to all the people who were "forced" to get jobs, 10 in all, and they agreed to meet with me in my office to discuss their progress. I thought I'd begin with the one person

I knew would have the biggest problem with the new law—James the doctor. It's rumored that one summer he faked sunstroke to get out of mowing the lawn. He looked it up in some medical journal and acted out the exact symptoms. Then after his father finished the lawn, he faked a miraculous recovery. He was actually admired for how good he was at being lazy. If anyone was going to fail at finding work, it was James. That is, unless he was pushing people down cliffs so he could give them medical attention and charge them afterward. The way things were going, that didn't appear to be beyond the people of this town.

James came in with a much different look on his face than when he had come in before. He actually seemed excited to talk to me. Of course, the cliff theory immediately came to my mind. "So, James. How are you doing?"

"Great. Thanks."

"Are you finding any work?"

"Sure."

I swallowed a lump in my throat. "What kind?"

"I sold some lemonade and juice and stuff. See?" He reached into his back pocket and pulled out two starbills. My mouth fell open. "Remember how it was so hot the other day? I guess people were pretty thirsty, huh?"

"You made two starbills selling drinks?"

"And change. Sold about 40 cups."

I smiled. "You're kidding me. That's great!"

"I just thought about what you said. About being a productive member of society and participating in the economy. So I figured I should do this."

"I'm impressed. So I guess you're gonna keep this lemonade thing going, huh?"

"Definitely. I hear it's gonna be a hot summer."

"Well, I'm sorry for ever doubting you. You really came through. I was beginning to think this new program wasn't working for anybody, but at least it worked for you."

"Yeah," he said.

"Well, I'll tell you what. Go on and keep doing what you're doing. In a few weeks I'll check to see if you're still making money. OK?"

"Sounds good."

James left, and I held my chin high. I felt like a father whose son just hit a home run to win the game. I imagined turning to the other parents in the stands, saying, "I taught him that swing."

* * *

Much to my delight, most of the interviews went just as well. Out of the 10 interviewees, only three were displeased with the new law. Five had gone out and gotten new jobs or figured out new ways to make money. A couple of them, like James, had never lifted a finger a day in their lives. But I guess with the right amount of incentive, people can produce. I began practicing the speech I would give before the U.S. Congress in 25 years: "Ladies and gentlemen, I have two words for you: Everybody Works!" (Applause.) "Thank you!" (More applause.) "Thank you . . ." (Standing ovation.) "Thank you . . ."

* * *

The first thing I did after the interviews was tell Scott, and he immediately took the wind out of my sails.

"James sold lemonade?" he asked.

"That's what he said."

"Do you believe him?"

"He had the money right there."

"But you know for sure that's how he got it?"

"I have no proof, no. You don't think he sold lemonade?"

He picked up a pipe from the table. He was slipping back into his Sherlocke Holmes mode again. It wasn't a real pipe—it was one of those you use for bubbles, but he claimed it helped him think. "That doesn't sound like James."

"I know it doesn't. That's what's so great."

"And the others. How did they get their money?"

"Different ways." I looked at him and grabbed the pipe out of his mouth. "Oh, come on! You think they're all lying?"

"Pardon me for raining on your victory parade, but it sounds suspicious," he said as he grabbed the pipe back. "I think I should investigate."

I guess he figured he was on a roll detective-wise. "I'm not paying you."

"I know that. I'll do this one for you on the house."

I rolled my eyes. He never did like the new law. I guessed this was his way of trying to prove it didn't work. He picked up his magnifying glass and hat and took off.

And when he opened the door, I heard some-one screaming.

CHAPTER 8

Jill's house was next to Scott's in Kidsboro, and that's where the screaming was coming from. Jill's finger was pointing at Marcy's nose, and Marcy wasn't backing away from it. They were both yelling at the same time, listening to nothing but themselves. Others were gathering around to watch the fracas, but Marcy and Jill didn't see these people either. All they were seeing was red.

"I never should've hired you!" Jill shouted.

"I wish I'd never asked you to!" Marcy replied.

"Fine. Then go ask Corey for a job. Start picking through our trash cans. I hear he needs a decorator for his kitchen!"

"If I knew what a jerk you'd be for a boss, I would've done that to begin with."

"*I'm* a jerk? You've been my employee for three weeks, and you may have just bankrupted us!"

"You take this dumb newspaper too seriously."

"Well, thanks to you, that might not be a problem anymore."

"I hope it does go bankrupt. At least you'll be human again."

This was too much for me to sit back and watch. I felt responsible for some of this, and the verbal zingers were getting way too personal. I stepped in. "Hey, hey. Wait a minute."

"Go away," Jill said to me.

"I'm quitting this town," Marcy said.

"Marcy—" I said.

"No, wait. I'm not quitting yet. I'm gonna stick around long enough to vote you out of office, then I'll quit." She left with heavy feet.

Jill turned away from me and headed back into her house. I debated going the other direction and letting her cool off, but I wanted to defend myself now. I opened the door. She was sitting at a table with her head resting on a stack of papers—the issue in which Corey was misquoted.

"Jill—" I whispered.

"*You're* the cause of all of this!" she shouted without looking up.

"You guys'll work this out."

"She was a good friend, Ryan. I slept over at her house when we were in *kindergarten!* I've *never* fought with her like this."

"That's why you'll be OK."

"Please! Let me call a city council meeting!"

75

"It's not the law, Jill. The program is working. We just need to work out a few of the kinks."

"You're putting the town before friendships."

"I'm not, I—"

Her head popped up like her neck was attached to a spring. "Then how come I just lost one of my best friends?" She brushed her hair away from her face. Her lips quivered, and she stared at me for an answer to this unanswerable question. She took a long, hard breath. "There are things that go on outside these woods, Ryan," she said.

"I know," I replied.

"Then maybe you should stop being a mayor so much and just be a kid." Jill laid her head back on the stack of papers.

"I'm sorry." I didn't know what else to say, so I turned away and left.

The crowd that had gathered to see the cat fight between Marcy and Jill had not yet dispersed. They all looked at me, searching for some look on my face that would tell them what had happened. Scott ran up to me and sensed that something had just happened.

"What's going on?" he asked.

"Nothing," I said.

"Well, hey," he began, excited. "Guess what I just saw?"

I looked at him as if to say, "I'm not guessing."

"I saw James coming out of Max's house."

I failed to catch his point, and he noticed this.

"Come on—James and Max? They're not friends. They're not even *close*."

"Scott, would you please get to whatever point you're trying to make."

"I think Max is up to something."

"So what's new?"

"No, I mean, with all these people suddenly making money. Like James. I think Max is responsible."

"You think he's hiring them for something?"

"I don't know. But it looks kinda possible, doesn't it?"

I hated to admit it, but this did sound like something both James and Max would do. "Let's go investigate," he said, leading the way.

* * *

I think Scott sensed that if he was going to uncover something here, he was going to have to do it primarily on his own. I did not want to find anything. I wanted James to be telling the truth.

We sneaked toward Max's house and watched from behind a tree. James was nowhere in sight. We tiptoed a little closer, making more noise than we would have if we had just walked, but that wasn't important. Scott was on the prowl. We were now behind the closest tree to Max's house, and we could hear voices from inside.

"Is that James?" I whispered.

"I can't tell," Scott said. The leaves crunched

under Scott's feet as he inched closer.

Suddenly the door swung open. He scurried back to the tree. James came out of the house. "It's due Monday," Max said to him from the inside. James had a thick book in his left hand.

"OK," James replied, like a servant to his king, and closed the door behind him.

"Let's get him," I said.

"Wait," Scott said. "Let's just follow him for a minute."

James went through the downtown and stopped at one of the two picnic tables that made up our "park." He sat down and opened the book. He pulled a pencil out of his pocket and began to work. Scott was ready.

"OK, let's go."

We pretended we were on our way to the other side of town and just happened to see our good friend James there.

"James!" Scott said with a pasted smile on his face.

James had no idea why Scott was stopping by to talk to him. "Hi."

"What are you doing?" Scott asked as he sat across from him at the picnic table. I slid in next to him.

"Just a little homework."

"Oh." Scott lifted the corner of the thick book from the table to read the title. "Algebra. Tough stuff. Especially for a sixth grader."

James pulled the book back and suddenly became very interested in his homework.

"You know, Ryan, I don't know any *sixth* graders in algebra. That's a seventh grade class, isn't it?"

"I think so," I said, knowing exactly what Scott was up to and playing along.

"I'm in an advanced placement class," James said, stuttering over every word. This was actually not that far from believable. James was definitely smart enough to be in an advanced placement class. The problem with him is that he would be too lazy to do all the work required. I didn't believe him, and neither did Scott.

"Oh, I didn't know that. But I guess I could've just asked the algebra teachers. I have them for math. In fact, maybe I'll ask them at school tomorrow."

"Well,"—James was thinking fast—"I'm not actually in the class. They didn't want me to be in a seventh grade class, you know, because I'm a sixth grader, but I'm doing the work at home. I have a tutor."

This was very good.

"I gotta go," James said as he quickly closed his book.

"But you just got here," Scott said.

"I know, but I just remembered something I gotta do." James spun out of his seat and practically ran away from us, stumbling over a tree root as he went.

"So what do you think?" Scott said.

I hated to admit this. "I think Max is paying him to do his homework."

"Pretty obvious."

"But that doesn't mean Max is paying *everybody*. Max doesn't have that much homework—and he's smarter than most of those kids. There's no way he'd *let* them do his homework."

"That's what investigations are for," Scott said, scratching his chin and raising his eyebrows.

At least *someone* was enjoying his job.

* * *

I felt obligated to go to Jill's trial, though I didn't really want to witness it. In my opinion, Jill didn't have much of a chance. The only thing she had going for her was the fact that she was defending herself, and Pete was the opposing lawyer. Pete was, of course, the worst lawyer in the history of the world, but he had court experience now, after botching David's case a month or so ago. There was always the remote possibility that he wouldn't be able to find the court-room, but now that he has court experience . . .

Corey was suing for 30 starbills, which was a lot. Nobody in Kidsboro had 30 starbills laying around, except Max, who probably had 30 starbills under his sofa cushion at home. Rumor had it that if Pete won, Max would get a third of the winnings. Ten starbills would be enough for him to live off for a pretty long time.

And Jill was right when she said that Marcy may have bankrupted her. Jill didn't have 30 starbills to pay. Obviously, she used her own real money (and her father's computer) to create the newspaper, so she didn't actually have to cease production. But this would mean that all the profits she made at the newspaper would go to Corey for a long, long time. Jill wouldn't have anything for living expenses. She would be no better off than James, the quack doctor. Plus, she had a business, and there was a paragraph in the city charter about paying special business taxes. She would end up owing the city a lot of taxes after a while.

The jury would not be thinking about that, though. They would probably be thinking about doing something cool. Like nailing the press.

The court was brought into session, and Pete made his opening statement. He basically just stated the facts—that the *Kidsboro Chronicle* was irresponsible for printing something that was not true, and that Corey was now having to go through public humiliation because of it.

Jill made her own opening remarks, admitting that it was a mistake, but that we all make mistakes, and that she would print a retraction, stating that Corey does not, in fact, decorate his room with garbage. She also questioned the amount Pete was asking for. "Thirty starbills? The paper doesn't make that in a whole year!"

I noticed a couple of people in the jury nodding their heads when she said this. Thirty starbills was too much. Jill had a good chance of getting the amount reduced to 15, or even five. Five she could handle.

Pete called his first witness. "I'd like to call Corey Hawkins to the stand." Pete and Corey had obviously rehearsed this. Corey pretended to be very upset at how people were treating him. He was practically in tears as he told a story about how somebody glued soda cans together to form a swan and put it in his front yard. It wasn't a pretty story, but the performance was so fake that I think it turned some of the jurors off. It was looking like Jill might have a chance. That is, until Pete called his second witness.

"I'd like to call Marcy Watson to the stand."

Marcy stepped up, ready to tell her story. The bailiff swore her in. "Marcy," Pete began, "how would you describe your relationship with Corey?"

Marcy was surprised by the question. "My relationship?"

"Yes. Are you friends?"

"Well—"

"Do you like him?"

She shrugged her shoulders. "I don't know."

"Have you ever had him over for dinner? Done homework together?"

"No."

"So you're not friends."

"No. I guess not."

"Are you enemies?"

"I wouldn't say that."

There wasn't very much space for anyone to move in the assembly hall, but what room Pete did have, he made use of right here. He began to pace in little 12-inch circles, like a buzzard ready to feast.

"But isn't it true that in the third grade you had a little . . . argument?"

"I don't know what you're talking about."

"An argument about a doll?"

Marcy's eyes went to the floor. She knew what he was talking about. "Marcy, didn't Corey steal your Baby Wetty Doll and throw it down the sewer?"

Marcy flipped. "Are you trying to say I did this on purpose?"

There was a murmur from the crowd.

"Just answer the question, please." He had been waiting to say that for years.

"That was years ago!"

"Answer the question."

"I forgot all about that."

"Yes, or no."

"Yes, but—"

"And didn't you say, Marcy, and I quote, 'I'll get you back for this if it's the last thing I do'?"

"I don't remember."

"Is it possible that you said that?"

"I guess."

"No further questions."

Marcy stood up. "I didn't do this on purpose. Why would I still care about that?"

The judge asked Marcy to sit down. I looked over at Jill, who had her head down. If the jury believed Marcy did it on purpose, they might just give Corey all the money he wanted.

Jill asked Marcy to come back up when it was her turn. She tried to make it clear that Marcy had no intention of getting back at Corey for something that happened in the third grade. I didn't know if it worked or not.

The lawyers made their closing statements, then left it to the five-person jury. After 10 minutes it looked as if the jury would be arguing for a while, so I left. Jill was outside facing the opposite direction from Marcy. They still wouldn't speak to one another. I couldn't look at Jill, either, as I passed her.

* * *

The jury came back in 45 minutes, and I honestly didn't have a clue as to what the verdict would be. I bit my lip as one of them read from the slip of paper he held in his hand.

"The jury finds for the plaintiff."

Corey won.

"For the full amount of the suit."

All 30 starbills. Corey and Pete gave each other high-fives, while Jill immediately left the room. I ran after her.

"Jill!" I shouted after her, and finally caught up with her.

"Go away," she said softly.

"Jill, I'm sorry."

She stopped suddenly, and I almost ran into her. She looked at me with her hands on her hips. "Thanks a lot!"

She took off, and I didn't follow her.

I was sitting in my office, staring at the wall, when Scott came running in. "You gotta see this," he said, and didn't wait for me to get up.

We ran to a park that was just on the other edge of the woods, outside of town. There was a gathering of about 20 people, some Kidsboro residents, some not. I wasn't quite sure what was happening, but Max and several of his friends seemed to be pushing five other kids (all Kidsboro residents) on the merry-go-round. But the riders didn't appear to be having fun, only the pushers.

"What are they doing?'

"Max and his friends have been pushing these guys on the merry-go-round for about three hours now, non-stop."

"Three hours?"

"It gets worse. About an hour ago they went into phase two. They forced them to eat greasy potato chips. A full bag each."

"*Forcing* them? How?"

"You tell me. Why do you think these guys owe anything to Max?"

"You think they all borrowed money from him?"

"I've got no proof, but it sure looks that way."

Scott left to go sneaking around a bit. No one noticed me as I walked a bit closer. The five boys on the merry-go-round were looking very green. There was also a large piece of cardboard with writing on it. As I studied it more, it seemed to be a sign asking for predictions on which kid would throw up first. No one had done so yet, but by the looks of the victims, it wasn't too far away. There was also another friend of Max's videotaping the entire thing and giving the play-by-play commentary.

I thought about what I could do. Since they were not within the Kidsboro city limits, there was nothing that I could do, legally. I had no authority over Max. We were both just kids in a park. But there had to be another way I could make him pay for this cruelty.

Scott ran up and handed me a piece of paper. "Look at this," he said. "I found it in James' book bag."

"What are you doing going through people's book bags?"

"It was open."

I looked at the paper. "What is it?"

"A loan contract between James and Max. Max

gave James a loan of 10 starbills at 50 percent interest, compounded monthly."

I quickly did some math in my head and soon figured out that James would owe Max about 33 starbills by the end of the summer. Max was the only one who could pay off 33 starbills. *Maybe Kidsboro needs a savings and loan,* I thought.

"And look at this right here," Scott went on, pointing to the bottom of the page. "It says that if James doesn't make monthly payments, then Max will determine how payment will be made."

"Meaning James will have to be his slave."

"Bingo."

"Meaning he will have to do his homework and play along with him and his friends while they put him on the vomit machine."

"Exactly."

"OK. Max can't get away with this." I stomped over to him. He was pulling a six-pack of soda out of a black box. He seemed happy to see me, which annoyed me a lot.

"Hey! My good friend Ryan! You're just in time. We're fixin' to go into phase three. The warm soda phase!" He laughed. "Won't that be the coolest!"

"I found this in James' book bag."

"What are you doin' goin' through people's book bags?"

"It was open."

Max looked at it and smiled. "Oh, yeah. One of my

little goodies. What a nice idea this turned out to be, huh?"

"You can't do this."

He didn't stop smiling. "I can't?"

"You can't make him pay back his loan by spinning him on a merry-go-round for three hours."

"Oh, but you know what? Strangest thing. Right here, in the contract. See that? That right there says I can."

"I don't care what this lousy contract says."

His smile disappeared. "The city charter states that all legal documents are binding. This is a legal document, signed by me, James, and a certified lawyer of Kidsboro."

I looked at it again. Pete's signature was at the bottom. Another person I needed to scold.

"According to this *legal* document, I can charge any interest rate I want, and I can collect it however I want."

He was right. He could make these kids spin until their eyeballs faced the back of their head, and I couldn't do anything about it.

"How many do you have under contract?" I asked, not wanting to know.

"Five," he said, smiling. He took off with the warm soda. "Hey, we're going into phase three. You're welcome to stay."

Five. And if memory served, that's exactly how many people whose lives were "saved" by the "Everybody Works" program.

* * *

The first thing I had to do was call a city council meeting. Whether it looked like a political move or not, I had to recall the new law. It wasn't working, and it threatened to destroy the town. I was headed over to Jill's office when Nelson grabbed me. He told me that two friends were going to court against each other. One boy was suing the other boy for breaking his remote control car. Nelson was right. People saw how well the lawsuit against Jill had gone, and they all wanted a piece of the action. Everybody's going to be suing everybody. I told Nelson we were having an emergency city council meeting, and he ran off to find the others.

* * *

As if that wasn't enough, I was about to go into Jill's office when Valerie came up to me. She handed me an envelope.

"I'm suing you," she said, and promptly left without an explanation.

I opened it up. It was one of those legal documents. It stated that I was being sued for discrimination. Apparently Valerie wasn't too happy about the way I voted people in. I realized immediately that this was her campaign strategy. A mayor who was about to be sued didn't look too good. And the election was in two days.

*   *   *

The city council met, and by a vote of four to one (Alice being the lone "nay"), we agreed to repeal the "Everybody Works" program. Everybody could go back to being themselves, living in their houses, while all the businesses in town go bankrupt because nobody's making any money.

*   *   *

I was planning on spending the rest of the day preparing for the debate, which was the next night, but when I got back to my office, I was too depressed to think about it. I guess Max was right. This wasn't a town. It was a bunch of clubhouses in the woods.

On Tuesday I wrote down the 10 things I would least want to be doing that night. Number one was getting dragged behind a car through a field of cactus. Debating Valerie in front of the whole town was number two.

The election was the next day, and I wasn't sure if I could turn the tide in one night. In a town of only 28 people (down from 29, after we banished Nick), you can pretty much figure out who's going to win if you simply know the people. I knew I had my own vote (unless Valerie was so good in the debate that she convinced me not to vote for myself), and I knew I had Scott's. He was, anyway, my friend. After that, I had no idea if I had any more votes. Max would vote for Valerie since he obviously had no regard for me whatsoever. Alice was mad at me for humiliating her about the David investigation. Jill was mad at me for ruining her life. Nelson was a possible vote. Then again, being Valerie's brother, he had to live with her wrath if he happened to be the vote that caused her to lose. I knew a few of the boys who would vote for Valerie, because they were secretly in love with her. I guess I can't count on all the girls being secretly in love with *me*, but that's a possibility.

All Valerie needed was 15 votes, and I could count six or seven that she definitely had already. Then, of course, I was sure she had quite a performance planned for the debates. Put Valerie on stage in front of a bunch of people and she could persuade an Eskimo to put central air conditioning in his igloo.

When I got to the meeting hall, I counted the people. A standing-room-only crowd of 28. This *would* have to be the event nobody missed, wouldn't it?

I sat in front, facing the crowd, and Valerie was already there, smiling at all the registered voters. She was dressed like she was going to church, and looked quite pretty, actually. Jill sat in front with us. She was chosen to be the host for the event.

Valerie stood up and showed her good sportsmanship by coming over to me and shaking my hand. She smiled sweetly and said, "Good luck, Mr. Mayor." She quickly looked around the room to see if anyone saw this generous gesture, then returned to her seat.

Jill began by welcoming everyone and introducing the participants. Then she asked us to begin with an opening statement.

Valerie stood and gave everyone a big smile.

There was a lot of applause. She stood at a stand in front and began. "Ladies and gentlemen, I have decided to run for this office not because I don't respect our current mayor—our mayor has run this town as best he can. He has done exactly what he thinks is best for us, and for that I respect him."

I hoped I wasn't the only one who could see how phony she was.

"But I also think, somewhere along the road, our mayor has lost touch with the people. He *wants* to do what's best, but he no longer *knows* what's best. And I believe I *do* know. Thank you."

There was scattered applause, then everyone looked at me. I was never told how this debate would go, so I hadn't really prepared an opening speech. I definitely didn't have anything as polished as the one I just heard, but I stepped to the stand.

"I also respect my opponent," I said, hoping people couldn't detect how phony *I* was. "And I respect her right to challenge me for this office. After this is over, if I'm reelected, I'll make sure regular elections are put into the city charter. But do you really think this town needs a different leader? I have always based my decisions on what I believe are the things that will help the town prosper. If you think I have done that, I'd appreciate your vote."

Again, there was scattered applause. I looked into the crowd at Nelson. He told me he was bringing a new invention—an applauseometer—to the debate.

A few people were huddled around him, looking at it. They were checking to see if Valerie's applause had been louder than mine, and I wondered too.

Jill then went ahead with questions. Her first question was how we planned to make the city better, if we were elected. Valerie, of course, started in on her "less rules" campaign, except she called it "more freedom to do as we choose."

"Our mayor actually tried to force people to do work. His 'Everybody Works' program should've been called 'Everything Works But This Program.'" Some laughter. "Of course, yesterday he repealed this law, but then again, he also knew there was an election coming up. How convenient!"

I figured she would use this.

"But let's be honest, people. The economy is in shambles. Businesses are going under, and it's not because people don't want to work. It's because there are no jobs out there. As your new mayor, I will start a program that will introduce new jobs into our community. And I promise that I will never tell you that you have to work or you'll lose your house."

Some applause. I could sense from the crowd that they liked this idea and, in fact, Valerie made it sound great.

When I got up, I responded to Valerie's "more freedom" thing and said that even though rules aren't something we like, they were still something we needed. I sat down. It was obvious Valerie received more applause after this segment of the debate.

Jill then asked a question about new ideas we might have for the coming year. I decided to take on Max here.

"There are people in this town who seem to be taking advantage of the freedom they do have. I consider that *crime*." I didn't mention any names, but everyone there knew who I was talking about. I even detected a smile from Max in the back. "I believe we should crack down on this stuff before it gets worse and people get hurt."

Little applause.

It was Valerie's turn, and she stood up confidently and smiled at me as she went to the stand, as if to say, "This is where I lock up the election."

She began. "I believe this town has a lot of potential. A lot of potential for growth, and learning, and for just being a place to have fun. But I don't think our current mayor realizes this potential as much as he should. I think we should be more open-minded about who we allow to become citizens of Kidsboro. In fact, our mayor is currently being sued for that very reason. He seems to show preferential treatment to his friends, and he doesn't even realize that his friends are all the same. We can have a *different* assortment of personalities here and, therefore, become a city of variety and new ideas."

My eyebrows raised. What was she going to suggest?

"For example,"—she glanced my way to make

sure I was listening carefully, and she had my full attention—"Luke Antonelli. I believe most of us know him."

Yes, everyone knew him. He was one of the biggest troublemakers in our school.

"I know for a fact that he would like to become a member of this town. My question is Why wouldn't he be allowed?"

I had a few hundred reasons, actually. I wasn't sure where she was going with this. No one in their right mind would want Luke Antonelli living next door to them.

She went on. "I believe that Luke has a lot to offer our town. For one thing, his father owns a swimming pool store. Luke has told me that if he were allowed to join us, he would get his father to give us a small used pool. Now wouldn't it be nice to have a public pool in our town?"

I looked into the crowd and saw some heads nodding. I couldn't believe this! She was promising pools!

"There are many others who can offer so much to our town. Jerry Wilmott, for instance."

Jerry Wilmott! He's a three-time convicted shoplifter!

She continued. "Jerry's mother works for the city and can get access to all the equipment and property within the city parks. Wouldn't it be nice to be able to go to the nearby baseball fields and play a game there any time we want? Under the lights, even! As a matter of fact, I think Kidsboro could field a pretty good team," she added with a playful chuckle.

By the time she finished answering the question, Kidsboro had a paintball field, an ice cream place, and a recreation area that included a pool table, basketball court, and refreshment stand. I had no idea how she could promise these things, but the crowd seemed to think she could. They were drooling faster with every word that came out of her mouth.

By the time my turn came up, there was nothing I could've said that would even get anyone's attention, much less change their vote. I pleaded with them not to allow this town to be filled with hoodlums, but they didn't seem to care. They wanted a pool.

The next day I went to the meeting hall and cast a vote for myself. I figured it might be the only one I'd get.

Twenty-eight votes is not a lot to count, so when the polls closed at 6:00 that night, we were all gathered in the meeting hall at 6:05 to hear the outcome. Alice counted the votes since she was the highest-ranking person in town, besides me, who was a city employee. Also, she was considered trustworthy by pretty much everyone. She read the small pieces of paper and made tally marks in her notebook. After a couple minutes, she rose and went to the front to make the announcement. Valerie and I were in the same seats we had sat in for the debates. Alice approached the stand. She cleared her throat, and the hall was immediately silent.

"The winner, by a vote of 25 to 3, is Valerie Swanson."

There was applause and some whooping and hollering from some of Valerie's most loyal fans. Valerie showed very little emotion, however. She smiled, and graciously came over to me and shook my hand.

"I always keep my promises, Ryan," she said before she went to the stand to address her town. Indeed, she had kept her promise. She promised she would take over the town—and it was hers.

* * *

I was actually a little bit excited by the fact that I got one more vote than I expected. From whom, I couldn't guess, but at least somewhere out there I had a fan I didn't know about.

For the next week I spent very little time in town. I cleared out my office the day of the election, and I went back a few times after that. But other than that, I pretty much stayed at home—my *real* home. Valerie seemed to have the city running pretty smoothly. I heard a rumor that she was going to put Luke Antonelli (and his pool) up for a vote soon, along with a few others.

I did make one trip to town that week. We have a church in Kidsboro. It's not a building, but rather an area next to the creek that runs along the edge of town. I go to real church every week—my entire family goes. When my mother remarried, she married a Christian man who brought us to church. I didn't like it too much at first, but during the following two years, I had really begun to enjoy it. I became a Christian myself a year after we started going.

The Kidsboro "preacher," a 10-year-old boy

named Joey, had a service for anyone who was interested. Joey was the second African American in Kidsboro, other than Max. Joey's father was a real pastor. He was the minister of the church where you could hear the service from the other side of town. The members of that church yelled and sang and had such a great time. Someday I would have to go there with Joey, just to see what was causing the ground to shake.

I'd been to only a couple services at the Kidsboro Community Church, and there had never been more than three people in attendance, including the preacher himself.

The service was usually about 15 minutes long. There was always a song, a short sermon, and the offering plate was passed, but no one ever put anything in it. Joey was always hopeful though. He never missed a week, either. He always had something to say.

His sermons were a little painful to watch. He tried to get himself riled up every now and then, just like his father did in the pulpit. He would yell something that could just as easily have been whispered. The problem was that Joey was just not that exciting. So when he tried to *sound* exciting, it just came across as annoying.

I was the only person there that day. Joey was glad to see me. He said he was sorry about the election and that he would pray for me. Oddly enough, this was kind of nice to hear.

Joey led the two of us in a chorus of "Seek Ye

First," which I knew. He wanted to try it in a round, but I told him that would be kind of weird since there were only two of us.

Joey then launched into a sermon. I never got much out of his sermons, because he never really said anything that I didn't already know. I knew all the stories and the morals to all the stories. Some weeks he would have sermons with outlines that went something like this:

I. Noah

    A. He was obedient.

        1. Be obedient!

    B. He loved God.

        1. Love God!

    C. God loved him.

        1. God loves you!

Not much of a life-changing message, if you know what I mean. But I appreciated Joey for trying, so every now and then I would sit through one of his services just to show my support.

This day he spoke about the Ten Commandments. I knew all of them already, so I kind of sat back and let him go through the list, smiling and nodding, but not getting a whole lot out of it.

Then he said something that struck me. He said, "Wouldn't it be a great world if everybody followed the Ten Commandments?"

How true! No stealing. No killing. No lying. None of that. The Ten Commandments—now there were some rules you didn't mess with.

I was so struck by that statement that I didn't really listen to the rest of the sermon. After he was finished, Joey prayed with his arms raised, then passed the offering plate. I took it and stared at it for a second. He wasn't quite sure what I was going to do with it, and neither was I. But then I reached into my pocket and took out 17 starbills—everything I owned—and placed it in the offering plate. He looked at the money like it was the Holy Grail. I patted him on the shoulder and said, "Thanks, Joey." He was still staring at the money when I left.

I'm not exactly sure why I gave everything I owned to the church. Maybe it was because the church was the last thing in Kidsboro that I felt I could have faith in.

* * *

School ended for the summer the following week. The first week we were out, it happened. Right out of the blue, the impossible occurred.

I was at the video arcade with Scott. We had been spending a lot of time together, mostly away from Kidsboro. Without me, I guess he didn't have any reason to be there either.

"You wanna play 'Laser Man'?" Scott asked. He knew I didn't. I wasn't a big fan of video games but would go there to watch him, the master of all video games. He stuck a quarter into the big box and punched a few buttons to get himself going. He spread his legs to get his balance and prepared for video battle.

Just then I noticed a boy in a leather jacket, glancing over at us. I couldn't see his face well, but every now and then I would look over and he would quickly turn the other direction. It was like he was staring at me, but didn't want me to know it. I tried to concentrate on the video game.

Just as Scott began level three, I heard footsteps behind us. I turned.

"Jim Bowers," he said, looking at me.

A lump settled in my throat. "W-W-W-What?"

"You're Jim Bowers," he said.

My leg was shaking uncontrollably. "You— You're mistaken. My name is Ryan."

"Gimme a break, Jim. I'd know you anywhere. What? In four years you've already forgotten me? Jake Randall."

I glanced at Scott to see what his reaction to all this was. He was half concentrating on the game, and half on me. I turned toward the machine. "I don't know what you're talking about," I said.

"What are you doing? Don't be an idiot; I know who you are."

Scott stepped in, probably because the guy was breaking his concentration. "Pardon me for being on earth, but you've got the wrong person. His name is Ryan Cummings."

"Ryan Cummings?" he said with a chuckle. "Get real, Jim. Stop the game. I know it's you."

I turned around, showing a little more anger than I probably should have. "Listen, I don't know what you're talking about. My name is Ryan, and this Jim is probably somebody that just looks like me, OK? Now would you please leave us alone?" I quickly became very interested in "Laser Man."

From behind me, I could sense he was in deep thought. "I don't know what you're doing; maybe you think I'm mad at you or something. I'm not. I'm OK. But I'm staying here with my grandmother until the end of the summer. I'll find out what's going on."

I watched him in the reflection of the video screen. He stood there for a second, then left. I exhaled.

"You know that guy?" Scott asked.

"No. Never seen him before."

I ran my fingers through my hair and took a deep breath. Jim Bowers. I hadn't heard that name in four years.

* * *

I tried to forget about the events at the video arcade, although I had a feeling it wasn't over.

Reports had it that things were going great in Kidsboro. All of Valerie's friends had become citizens. Somehow she got her pool, and it was the hot spot.

It was three feet deep and only 15 feet in diameter, but she packed them in there like sardines. Last I heard she was working on the volleyball court next. I couldn't imagine that she wouldn't get it.

I read a lot of books in my bedroom that week. Before we started the town, my summers were always spent reading alone in my bedroom. I would read about 20 books a summer. So in a way it was kind of nice to get back to that.

I would take trips into town just to see what was going on, but I'd never spend more than a few minutes there. Nobody said a lot to me as I passed them on the streets. I guess they didn't want to disturb my grieving process, or maybe they felt guilty for not voting for me. Whatever the case, I didn't feel much like a part of the community anymore. But I still had my books.

I was reading a good one when my mom told me I had a visitor. I went to the front door and looked through the screen. It was Jill.

"Hey," she said softly, smiling.

"Hey," I replied.

She shrugged, because I guess she hadn't rehearsed anything to say on the way there. "Whatcha doin'?"

"Reading. What are *you* doing?"

"Just thought I'd stop by. Haven't seen you in a while."

"Yeah." I looked out at the front porch swing and motioned to it. We sat down and I continued my thought. "I haven't spent a whole lot of time in town, really. Been reading a lot."

"I know," she said, pushing her hair away from her eyes. I was wondering if she had a point to this visit, but it didn't matter to me if she didn't. It was nice to simply see her.

"Marcy and I made up."

I thought there was a slight tone of forgiveness in her voice, and I eased up a bit. "Good."

This was not her point. She had another one. "So have you decided you don't want to be our friend if you can't be our mayor?"

This was not the point I had expected. I had expected one about a thousand times less blunt. She backed off when she saw me practically swallow my own tongue.

"I'm sorry. I shouldn't have said that. I know you're just—depressed, or whatever." She looked at me deeply, like she was trying to sense what I was feeling. "You feel like you're losing your town?"

By this point I had pretty much recovered from the first question, so I answered her. "I guess, a little bit."

"Well, you're not. We miss you. And we need you."

"You need me? Why?"

"I don't know . . . There's just something not right about everything when you're not there."

"You mean, it's a lot more fun when I'm not there," I said.

"Oh, Valerie's done some good things; I won't

lie. The pool's a blast. She's got about a hundred other ideas too. The place is gonna be Disneyland by the time she's through. She's even gotten a few people new jobs in the rec area she's building. But . . . it doesn't have the same, I don't know, *feeling* to it. We used to be such a family, you know? Well, the stuff that's been happening lately has kinda stunk, with me and Marcy and all that. But still, deep down, we were all friends, and we liked being around each other."

"And now?"

"Now? Well, as an example, Luke Antonelli's planning on moving next to Nelson. And Nelson's scared of him. He doesn't even want to live there anymore. He says he's gonna build another house somewhere else. And two of Valerie's friends had a fist fight the other day. Stuff like that never happened before. Makes me think it's because you're not around."

"I'm surprised you say that. I thought you'd be thrilled to have Valerie as your mayor. No lawsuits. She probably lets you print whatever you want in the paper—"

"Sure, but . . . I'd rather have you."

"Really?"

She moved her hair away from her face again and blushed a little. She looked at me. "*I* was your third vote." She cocked her head and chuckled.

I chuckled back because I never would've guessed that. "Why?" I asked.

"Because you were right—I should never have printed that story about David's dad. And you were right about David being innocent. And even though it didn't work out the way you wanted it to, that jobs program was something you thought would be a good thing for the town. And if we would've given it more time, I think it probably would have. You're always thinking of the town first. You're always doing whatever's right. You're the only person I've ever known who does that. And I want somebody like that as my mayor."

"But I lost."

"Come back anyway."

I thought about it for a second, and the next logical question came to my mind. "What am I gonna do for a living?"

"I don't know. You can work with me. Be my sports editor. We've got a volleyball court coming, you know."

We laughed for a second, then decided we had other things to talk about. We sat and talked until the sun went down.

I decided Jill was right about coming back and being a productive member of society, so I went back to town. But I still wanted to ease back into it. I figured I would take a job in which I wouldn't have to do any work. The perfect job immediately came to mind: I would work for Scott's detective agency!

Scott was excited about having me as an employee, not just because he had his best friend with him, but because he liked the idea of being my boss. Of course, he didn't have any real orders to give me, but every now and then he would make something up. "Wipe off my magnifying glass," he would say.

I was pulling up weeds in front of the agency when I saw someone approaching in swim trunks. I couldn't believe my eyes. It was Bruce Haines, the biggest bully in school, and probably the only person in the world I could truly call an enemy. He had seen me and felt he had to pay his respects.

"Cummings!" he said, smiling like he was my best friend. "Thought you quit this place."

"I just . . . had a little vacation."

"Well how about a little swim?"

I didn't like being in the same zip code as Bruce, much less a place that introduced the possibility of drowning.

"No thanks."

"Oh, come on."

"I'm gonna stick around here."

"Suit yourself," he said and started to leave. As if he regretted missing a perfect opportunity to pound me, he flicked his towel at me and stung my legs before he was out of reach.

After he was gone I went inside to see Scott. "What is Bruce Haines doing here?"

"Oh, yeah," he said, asking himself the same question. "He just made it in last week."

"What good could possibly come out of having Bruce here?"

"None. But he's here anyway."

"He was going to the pool."

"Yeah," Scott said. "I don't go to the pool anymore. Valerie's friends always hog it. And they splash water in your face and dunk you and stuff."

"What about everybody else? Do they go to the pool?"

"No. All the original people kinda stay away from Valerie's friends. Pardon me for being blunt, but nobody really likes 'em."

My heart sank. I had to go to the pool and see this for myself.

* * *

Just as Scott said, Valerie's friends were the only ones there. They seemed to be having fun, doing stunts and tricks they would never be able to do in a regular city pool with paid lifeguards. There wasn't an original member of the town in sight.

I was about to go back to Scott's place when I spotted something out of the corner of my eye. It was Valerie, watching her friends in the pool. She looked worried, as if she knew she was losing her grip on things. She turned and saw me. We stared at each other for a second, and for the first time I found myself feeling sorry for her. I wanted to help her, if not for her sake, then for the sake of the town.

I walked over to her, and we watched her friends in the pool for a few seconds. She didn't look at me, as if it was illegal for us to be talking to one another.

She finally broke the silence. "I appreciate your concern, but don't worry. I'm gonna fix this." She left quickly.

* * *

Valerie called for a meeting, and the entire town

gathered for it. The meeting hall had never been this packed. It normally held about 30 people, and that's with stuffing people everywhere. Today there were 35. All 28 pre-Valerie members of the town, plus seven of Valerie's friends. A few people stood outside with the door open.

No one knew why the meeting was called, but everyone (except maybe Valerie's friends) was aware that there was a problem in the town. We figured this would be Valerie's solution for it. Valerie stood up on stage and got everyone's attention. She was all smiles, like everything was just peachy.

"Thanks, everybody, for coming. I won't keep you long; I have just one announcement. I've decided we should have something to celebrate the new era of Kidsboro."

(Of course, this meant the era that started when she got me out of the way.) "We've had a lot of newcomers recently, and it doesn't seem like we know each other very well. So I think we should have a get-together. So this Thursday we're going to have a campfire."

This was met with a few smiles. Other people exchanged looks and shrugged their shoulders as if to say "I guess there are worse ideas."

Valerie went on. "It'll be a time just to get to know one another. We'll have some organized games, and each of us will bring hot dogs and marshmallows." (Valerie's friends suddenly paid attention—

food was involved.) "And at some point we'll all introduce ourselves and get to know one another."

Most of the crowd seemed to approve of the idea, and Valerie sensed this. However, I needed to step in here. I raised my hand. Valerie saw me. "Yes, Ryan?"

"I really like the idea of getting together like this, but to be honest, I'm not sure a campfire is such a good idea. It's been really dry here lately, and there's a lot of brush around. We could accidentally set the woods on fire. That's why it was always in the city charter that we couldn't have fires."

I looked at her face and immediately knew I should've waited until after the meeting to bring this to her in person. She was never going to let me show her up in front of the whole town. "I understand your concern, Ryan. But first of all, the city charter has been rewritten a little over the past couple weeks. I'll make sure you get a copy of that. Second, Bruce Haines, who is standing in the back there"—we all turned around, and he waved—"is a very experienced camper and knows how to contain a fire. I don't think there should be any problems." She looked around as though she had answered my concern sufficiently and was ready to move on to other questions. There were none, and she dismissed us.

I'm not sure what she expected to happen at the campfire. I imagine she had dreams of people weeping and holding hands around the campfire while singing "Kumbayah." Luke Antonelli and Scott

Sanchez locked in an embrace of unity? I think it was a good idea to try to bridge the gap between the two groups of people in town, but I didn't see it happening. I figured I should show my support for Valerie by actually attending, at least for a little while. But I was not in the mood to bond with Bruce Haines.

* * *

The night was perfect. The sky was clear, and the stars were bright. There was a cool breeze blowing so that when the fire started going, it would provide just the right amount of heat to make us all comfortable. Bruce had already picked the spot for the fire—a place in the middle of town. Everyone arrived with food (even the bullies, which surprised me). People had marshmallows, hot dogs, buns, potato chips, dip, soda, cookies, and lots of other things. Everyone seemed to be taking this seriously. This was a great sign for Valerie who, I knew, had to be nervous.

We all ate, and the groups sort of naturally separated themselves. Valerie's friends were huddled in one group on one side of the fire, away from everyone else. There was some interaction, but it was limited. At one point I saw Luke Antonelli help put ketchup on Nelson Swanson's hot dog. Valerie saw it and smiled. This was quite a victory for her, I knew. She must have had a talk with Luke beforehand.

I sat next to Scott. We ate, but talked little. We

both kept a close eye on Bruce and friends, because we didn't trust them to be nice for any length of time.

Near the end of dinner, Valerie brought us all closer to the fire and suggested that we introduce ourselves. We were to say our name and what position we held in town.

"I'm Valerie Swanson," she began, "and I'm the mayor." She chuckled artificially, very proud of being able to say that.

We went around the circle. "I'm Ryan Cummings, and"—everyone waited to see what I would say here, and how I would say it—"I work for Scott, here, at his detective agency." I tried to say that with all the pride that I could muster, but it just didn't sound right. Bruce and friends chuckled.

Then we got to them.

"I'm Bruce Haines, and I'm the town drunk."

This was met with hilarious laughter from his group, but no one else. Valerie was a little bothered by it, but put on a straight face.

"Bruce is going to take my place as the town lawyer," she said.

"Oh, yeah," Bruce said, "That's right. I'm doing that on the side."

More laughter from his crew.

The introductions continued.

"I'm Luke Antonelli. Pool maintenance."

More laughter. This was hardly a real job. Then again, neither was being Scott's assistant.

Bruce and his gang of laughing hyenas continued, each making up a position and receiving a lot of laughs for doing so.

After the introductions, Valerie suggested we play a game. As everyone was scurrying around to prepare for it, Scott and I took the opportunity to leave. I had put in my appearance, showing I supported and approved of our new mayor and her harebrained—I mean, *good* ideas.

* * *

Scott and I talked in his house for a while. As we did, we heard encouraging sounds from the campfire area. People were laughing and having fun. I couldn't believe it, but Valerie's idea seemed to be working. She had brought together two groups of people that I never thought could've been brought together. "So what if this works out?" Scott asked.

"What do you mean?"

"Will you be happy or sad?"

"I'll be happy," I replied, and meant it. "Maybe Valerie knows what's she's doing. If it works, we've all made some new friends, and the town is better for it."

We sat for a little while longer, listening to the sounds coming from the campfire. Just as I was contemplating going back to camp to get a refill of my drink, we heard a noise that didn't sound encouraging. It was a scream!

Both of us dropped our cups and ran outside. There were a few more screams as we approached the campfire. Nelson was running toward his house like he'd just seen a bear.

"What's going on?" I shouted.

"They're going crazy!" was all he could say as he kept running.

We ran as fast as we could toward the campfire. Several people were backed up against a house, scared as if they were being rushed at by angry wolves. Then I saw what they were so afraid of. Bruce and Luke were holding burning sticks, poking them at people.

Bruce was waving his torch and laughing. Luke rushed to Pastor Joey and came within inches of burning his face. Everyone screamed. They were paralyzed with fear, unable to move for fear that if they attracted attention to themselves the two boys would pick them as their next target.

"Come on, everybody! I'm not gonna hurt you. Come over here and let me show you how friendly I can be." Bruce waved his torch wildly, and some fire fell to the ground. "This is supposed to be a town where everybody trusts everybody else, right? Well, come on, you can trust me. We're all brothers here, right?"

Luke went over to a group of people and again scared the daylights out of them. The rest of Bruce's crew were getting some big laughs out of this.

Valerie was standing to the side and realized she was responsible for doing something about this. She stepped forward. "Bruce, stop it! Luke! Cut it out, right now! Put down the torches!"

Bruce chuckled and said, "Uh oh, Luke. Look out. Our mayor is telling us what to do."

Luke joined him gleefully. "Yeah, we'd better obey or she's gonna throw us in jail!"

"I mean it, you guys!"

"Oh," Bruce said, "she *means* it! Luke, I didn't know she *meant* it. I guess we'd better *mean* it, too."

With that, Bruce rushed at her with anger and poked the fire close to her stomach. Everyone screamed. Valerie backed away from him, but he kept after her. I've never seen such fear in anyone's eyes as I saw in Valerie's.

"Come on, Mrs. Mayor. I heard somewhere you *liked* playing with fire."

She started backing away more quickly, but then he lunged at her. In dodging the flame, she fell. He came right at her with the torch!

Without thinking, I ran toward them. The flame was inches from her stomach. Just as he turned to see me, I dove at the torch, knocking it out of his hand. He jumped on top of me, and we wrestled on the ground. Luke saw what was happening to his friend and dropped his torch and ran to help. He tried to pull me away from him. Scott ran over and tackled Luke, sending him sprawling to the ground.

Bruce was much stronger than me and had me pinned. Just as he was about to send his fist through my skull, he glanced to his right. His mouth dropped open. The fire had spread, and a house was in flames!

We suddenly forgot about beating each other up and gazed at the fire, which was already burning out of control.

"Get off!" I yelled and pushed Bruce off of me.

"Scott!" I shouted. "Go to Nelson's house; he's got a fire extinguisher!"

He ran to get it.

"Alice, go to my house and call 911!"

She obeyed.

"You people!" I pointed to a group. "Find some buckets or something and get water out of the pool and dump it on these flames!"

They all scurried off.

"You guys!" I shouted at Bruce's gang. "Help me stomp this out!"

Everyone took off their sweaters and shirts and tried to smother the flames. I frantically stomped on the ground. The fire had climbed all the way up the wall of a house and was making its way along the roof.

Scott came back with the fire extinguisher, and I took it from him and sprayed. The fire died wherever I hit it, but it had spread too far already. The house was consumed by flames.

A dozen people came back with glasses, buckets, hats, and anything else that would hold water, and began to pour it on the flames. But it was like trying to stop a tidal wave with a garbage can lid.

The spray ran out of my fire extinguisher, and we had nothing left to do. It was getting dangerous just being there, so I shouted to everyone to clear the area. We backed away and headed to the edge of the woods. We watched the flames from a hundred feet away, and waited for the fire department to get there.

The fire department got there in five minutes, but had some problems getting back into the woods, so it was 10 minutes before they were able to do anything to the flames. By that time, four houses were already consumed by fire.

* * *

We got a pretty stern talking to from the fire department. Scott told them what had happened, and the fire chief took Bruce and Luke aside and lectured them for a while. Four houses were burned to the ground and two more were damaged. No one was hurt, though. Everyone just kind of wanted to go home, take a bath, fall asleep, and forget about this night.

I wanted to go home too, but on my way I saw Valerie. She was sitting on a stump, alone. She was shivering with a blanket draped around her. She looked in the direction of the burned houses, but probably saw nothing but the memory of a flame being shoved into her face. I sat on the ground next to her.

"Are you OK?" I asked.

She nodded. Just about everyone else had gone by

this point, and all we could hear were the crickets chirping as if nothing had happened.

"Maybe you oughta get home," I said.

She nodded again. I guess she didn't feel much like talking. Neither did I.

"Thank you," she said suddenly. "And I'm sorry."

Probably the two hardest things she's ever had to say to anyone, and she accomplished them both in one sentence.

"That's OK," I replied.

We sat for a few more seconds, then she began again. "I'm resigning."

This shocked me, even under the circumstances. "This is your town. I'm giving it back."

"Are you sure?" I said, not knowing what else to say.

"Yes." She stood up and was now ready to go home. "Will you start rebuilding the houses tomorrow?"

"We'll do something tomorrow, I'm sure."

"OK. I'll be here." Valerie started to leave.

"Valerie," I said, and she turned around. "You did some good stuff. The rec center, that's great. You did one thing I didn't do. I was trying to force people into jobs that didn't exist. But you *created* jobs. I'm gonna use that."

"Thanks."

"I might need you in the future. You know, to help me brainstorm ideas."

"Sure." She gave me a half smile and left.

I got ready to leave myself, but then I saw that I wasn't the last person there. Jill was looking at her house, which was one of those that had burned down. She looked as if she were on the verge of tears.

"The very first issue of the *Chronicle* was hanging up on the wall of this house," she said tearfully. "Now it's gone."

I didn't know what to say, so I just patted her on the shoulder. She didn't react, as if she didn't even know I was standing there.

"Come on; I'll walk you home," I said.

She looked at me, then we turned and walked toward our real homes.

"Pretty wild night, huh?" she said.

"That it was."

"Guess I'll be starting from scratch tomorrow."

"Well, as for your house," I said, "don't worry about it. You've got insurance."

The next day I informed Max that he owed four people new houses, and he informed me that he knew this. He had to cough up about 80 starbills to pay for all of it. He was muttering under his breath as he filled a wheelbarrow full of wood and headed for the middle of town. The look on his face was all I needed to see. Justice was served after all.

I put Max back up for another vote before the City Council. I thought the others would feel, like me, that what he did to those kids on the merry-go-round was grounds for banishment. They disagreed, saying that he had a legal contract, and we had to honor that. Plus, we needed wood.

I had given it a shot.

* * *

A week later the town held a new election, and I

was unanimously voted in as mayor. It wasn't a terribly glorious victory since there was no one opposing me, but it was sweet anyway.

Bruce and the rest of Valerie's friends told her that they weren't interested in coming back to town, so keeping them out was not an issue. I had been afraid this was going to have to be my first act as mayor.

Within the next month, I would get the rec center going. We had a pool table/Ping-Pong table donated by a kid's parents, and that became the featured activity there. You could also use other sports equipment in a room next to it. I made it so that people who used the facility had to pay a small monthly fee, just like a real health club. The fees would then help pay any employees who worked there. Marcy was the first employee and enjoyed taking care of the place. She handed out equipment and refreshments, and kept the Ping-Pong players on a time limit. She was very happy with her new position.

City Council also voted on more government jobs. People were placed in positions where they raked leaves (a must in the fall when you're in the woods) and built "streets" made out of thin pieces of plywood so that people could ride their bikes up to their houses. Kidsboro suddenly seemed like a breath of fresh air.

* * *

But the first thing I did when I was reelected

mayor was to persuade David Smith to once again be a citizen of our town. And he accepted.

He was thrilled to be back. He moved into the same house he'd had before, and everyone introduced themselves. Some even apologized for accusing him of something he didn't do.

David decided on his job as well. He decided he wanted to work with Jill at the newspaper. He actually had some experience working on a school newspaper at his old school. Jill was more than happy to have him, since she was running out of ideas for news.

At the end of the day David came into my office and told me about his first day on the job. "I had a good time," he said. "Jill's really nice, ya know, and she let me write this article on how it feels to be a new citizen."

"Great."

"I even put a part in there about you. About how you believed in me, and stuff."

"Well . . ." I blushed. "You're easy to believe in."

"Anyway, I just wanted to come by and say thanks and that it's nice to be here."

"I'm glad you're with us," I said. He started to leave, then turned back. "You wanna know something?"

"What?"

"My dad . . . he really is in jail."

I felt it a deep honor that he would trust me enough to tell me this. It almost made me want to share my own secret, just to show him that I trusted him as a friend too. But I didn't. I couldn't.

Instead, I looked into his eyes and said, "I don't care."

He smiled, and turned toward the door.

"Welcome back, David," I said.

"Welcome back, Mr. Mayor."

THE END